"Jennifer Bohnhoff's *When Duty Calls* takes a moment from New Mexico's involvement in the Civil War and makes it flesh-and-blood real. The dual storylines will keep readers engaged and hoping Jemmy and Raul will eventually meet. A great fit for the classroom and beyond."
~ Caroline Starr Rose, author of *May B.*

"Jennifer Bohnhoff writes historical fiction that grabs readers with the action and characters so they enjoy learning the history."
~ Chris Eboch, author of *The Well of Sacrifice*

BOOK 2 OF
REBELS ALONG THE RIO GRANDE

The WORST ENEMY

by
Jennifer Bohnhoff

Illustrated by Ian Bristow

ISBN: 9781951122645 (paperback) / 9781951122652 (ebook)
LCCN: 2023934474
Copyright © 2023 by Jennifer Bohnhoff
Cover illustration © 2023 by Ian Bristow
Interior illustrations © 2023 by Ian Bristow
Map illustrations © 2023 by Matt Bohnhoff

Printed in the United States of America.

Kinkajou Press
9 Mockingbird Hill Rd
Tijeras, New Mexico 87059
info@kinkajoupress.com
www.kinkajoupress.com

Content Notice:
This book describes scenes of war and battle that may be traumatic for some readers.

This book is set in a period of U.S. history when modern values on human rights and racial equality did not exist. The book depicts the practices and concepts of racial and social inequality. These practices are not right today, and they were not right at the time when this story is set. The material is presented for historical accuracy and the author and the publisher condemn these practices in all their forms, whether in history or today.

ACKNOWLEDGEMENTS

Many, many thanks to my critique buddies, Michele Hathaway, Susan Metallo, Diane Mittler, and Christine Ottaviano Shestak, who picked and prodded and helped me make this a much better book. Each of these brilliant women are fabulous authors in their own right, and I look forward to promoting their books some day soon. Also, I am deeply indebted to my publisher, Geoff Habiger, who believed in this story and made both me and my characters better people.

DEDICATION

In Memory of Ken Dusenbery, U.S Army veteran of the Vietnam War, Civil War reenactor, and patient educator. I was privileged to be among the thousands who learned about the little details of service during two different wars through his guidance and his stories.

BATTLE OF

Apache Creek

Santa F

Apache Canyon

Santa Fe

✕

Johnson's
Ranch

Chivington's March

◀— — — — —

GLORIETA PASS

N

Pidgeon's Ranch

Trail

Pecos
Pueblo

Kozlowski's
Ranch

1 mile

1 kilometer

Glorieta Mesa

Table of Contents

"What is the position of New Mexico? The answer is a short one. She desires to be let alone. In her own good time she will say her say, and choose for herself the position she wishes to occupy in the new disposition of the new disrupted power of the United States."

Santa Fe Gazette
May 11, 1861

"Boys, I'm the worst enemy you have."

Henry Hopkins Sibley.
Sibley had resigned his commission in the U.S. Army and was leaving New Mexico territory by stagecoach when he shouted this to Union soldiers in Albuquerque's Old Town Plaza.

CHAPTER ONE
A HILL OF BEANS

Jemmy Martin
South of Socorro, New Mexico
February 23, 1862

Jemmy Martin looked at the boy cradled in his arms. "I sees lights up ahead, Willie. We's almost there."

"Home?" The drummer boy's face glowed grey in the twilight.

Jemmy's throat tightened. "We's still in New Mexico. Do you remember? You broke your arm two days ago? In the battle for Valverde Ford?"

Willie's dark eyes stared uncomprehendingly at Jemmy, who shook, both with emotion and fatigue. He'd been marching—no, staggering and stumbling—for

1

twelve hours. "Just hold on, Willie. This town ahead— it's named 'Socorro.' I's told it means 'help' in Mexican, and that is what we are gonna get. For you and all the wounded."

Jemmy set his jaw and tried to hold in his tears. Ten months ago, he'd been toiling behind the plow that Golphin and Griffith, the family mules, dragged through the field when he saw a dust cloud forming. It had been Drew, Jemmy's older brother, who came over the rise and pulled back on the reins, making his mount sidle and dance. "We fired on Fort Sumter on April twelfth!"

"Fort what?"

"Sumter! In South Carolina! The war we's been waiting for's finally begun!" Drew dug his heels and the horse bolted down the road. Jemmy watched him go, then shook his head and went back to the ploughing. He didn't give a hill of beans about who was firing on who back east. He had a field to plow. But he should have cared. His brother was going to sign himself up as a packer, who'd ride along with the Confederate Army's supply wagons. Worse, Drew had sold Golphin and Griffith to the Confederate Army. When Drew had slipped out of camp and returned home, abandoning the mules, Jemmy had felt responsible for staying with them and returning them home. But he'd never found the opportunity, and now here he was in New Mexico, the land his father hated. Jemmy had lost the mules the night before the Battle at Valverde Ford, the same battle in which Willie's arm had been broken. If he ever made it back to San Antonio, Pa was going to tan his hide for losing the family's two mules. What was he going to think about Jemmy bringing home this orphaned boy instead?

Jemmy carried Willie into a town of mud houses huddled around a dusty central square. Light glowed from open doorways and a few high, narrow windows. Jemmy stepped into the one that the Confederacy had requisitioned to be their hospital. He laid Willie on a mattress near a beehive-shaped fireplace in the corner of the room, then stretched out his back and straightened his arms, letting the feeling come back into them. "There," he said, "it's done."

Willie opened his eyes and stared up at him, a sad smile lifting one corner of his mouth. "Oh, Jemmy! Do you not know? It has just begun."

CHAPTER TWO
THINKING IS BELIEVING

**Cian Lochlann
Denver, Colorado Territory
Ten Months Earlier
Wednesday, April 24, 1861**

Cian Lochlann scuffled his feet, sending clouds of dust whirling along Blake Street. *T'inkin' is believin'*, Cian's Mam had said as they stepped off the boat onto a Boston pier back in 1847, when he was only two years old. She'd believed America was the land of opportunity, and that the family would prosper. But things hadn't turned out that way. First, Cian's Da disappeared and was presumed murdered, then his Mam died of typhus. Orphaned and alone, Cian was left to scrounge what living he could in a town that had grown tired and intolerant of their poor Irish immigrants. So, in 1859, when Cian heard that gold had been discovered in Colorado the previous year, he'd left Boston, determined to start a new, more honest life. That new life turned out to be no more secure and no more honest than the old one. Disenchanted and disheartened by two hard and luckless winters, he'd come down from the hills, looking for a job in a mercantile or livery stable that would offer a few coins and a corner to sleep in. After two days, he'd had no luck. His empty stomach rumbled.

Cian stopped and tilted his head, listening to angry voices somewhere off to the east. He smiled. Shouting could become a riot, and riots were an opportunity to grab food from a shattered shop window. As hungry and discouraged as he was, Cian was willing to slip back into his old ways. He trotted up G Street and turned onto Larimer, where he found himself at the back of an angry crowd. Cian sidled up to a man in a red flannel shirt and dungarees.

"Trouble?"

The man spit out a fountain of brown tobacco juice, then jerked his head toward a log building on the north side of the street. A sign hanging from the eaves said, 'Wallingford and Murphy, Mercantile.'

"Look what them jackasses hauled up their flagpole."

Cian squinted into the bright, cloudless sky at a red flag with a white X spangled with blue stars crossing from the corners. "And 'tis?"

"A Confederate flag, you ignoramus. Wallingford and Murphy are both transplanted southerners. 'Seceshes.' Colorado Territory's Union and intends to stay that way."

"Jaysus! Think they are going to loot the place?" Cian didn't care about either the Union or the Confederacy. He didn't understand what they were fighting about. That didn't stop him from wanting to grab some food and drink when the crowd surged into the store.

"Could be. Here." The man handed Cian a rock. It was weighty, and big enough to fill his palm. Just hefting it in his hand made his blood pound and his mouth water.

"Lookie there." The man jerked his chin towards a man climbing the hitching rail in front of the store. Transfixed, Cian watched the man swing himself onto the roof. The man was broad shouldered, like Cian's Da had been. The same dark mustache reached past both sides of his mouth. *This*, Cian thought, *is a man of action. He does not hesitate: He seizes an opportunity and squeezes all the luck out of it. He is the kind of man I'm looking to follow.*

Cian cheered with the crowd as the man hauled down the flag and ripped it to shreds, tossing the tattered pieces like party streamers.

"Now! Go!" The man next to Cian gave him a shove. He stumbled forward as the crowd surged towards the store and threw his rock when the crowd started pelting the building. The sound of breaking glass made his stomach groan in anticipation. Short as he was, Cian couldn't see what was happening, but he heard the heavy thud of shoulders slamming into the door, and then the splintering of wood.

The crowd pressed forward, carrying Cian along with it. Just as he got to the door, he hesitated, the sixth sense that he had honed during those dangerous days on the streets of Boston tingling. He glanced over his shoulder and saw men with badges turning the corner. Cian backed through the crowd and slipped into the shadows in the narrow alleyway next to the store.

A shot rang out. Cian dropped to the ground and flung his arms protectively over his head. The crowd reeled and screamed, just on the edge of panic, and for a moment Cian was afraid that they would stampede down the alley, trampling him. He looked up. Across the street, five heavily armed men accompanied the Town Marshal, whose badge gleamed in the sun.

"Time to go home, boys. Break it up," the Marshal shouted. The crowd scattered. In a matter of moments, only the Marshal and his men remained in front of the store. The Marshal craned his neck, looking up at the man who stood defiantly on the roof, his hands on his hips. "You want to tell me what you're doing up there?"

The man held up a shred of the Confederate flag. "Cleaning trash off the roof."

The Marshal nodded. "Do not hurt yourself getting down." With a quick jerk of his head, he moved his men back from where they'd come. Cian scrambled to his feet and stepped out of the shadows to wait by the hitching rail.

"Hoy, mister! I saw what you did!"

"Did you now? Good lad!" The man swung down to the street and stuck out his hand. "Samuel Logan."

Cian smiled broadly and pumped Logan's hand. This was the chance he'd been waiting for. "Cian Lochlann at your service, Mr. Logan, sir, and pleased to be making your acquaintance. Would you be needing a man right now?"

"As a matter of fact, son, I could use a few more men. Come, I will introduce you to the company." Logan took Cian by the elbow and guided him back down G Street.

Company, Cian thought, smiling to himself. *Mary, mother of Jaysus! I am going into business!* "And what kind of company would you be meaning, sir?"

"Cavalry," Logan answered, "and we don't even need our own mounts! The U.S. Government is going to supply them."

Cian swallowed down the lump of dread that formed

in his throat. He'd never been on a horse's back and sure didn't want to try it now. As they turned the corner onto Blake Street, a rough looking bunch of down-and-out miners and ne'er-do-wells hailed Logan. Cian felt his sixth sense tingling for the second time that day. He looked around as the rowdy men gathered close to shake Samuel Logan's hand, saw the passing of a flask, and knew these were not the men who were going to lead him into a new, more honorable life.

Cian backed away. It was time to go back to the South Clear Creek Mining District. He wasn't fond of the men there, either, but they looked safer than this lot. The question was, would the three men he'd left behind allow him to return after he'd told them they were all big-talking ne'r do wells when he'd left? They'd almost gotten into a fist fight, and Cian had stomped off in a huff, vowing never to see any of their pug-ugly faces. Now, he intended to do just that.

Cian walked north, the noise of Denver fading behind him. He sniffed and thrust his chin out. "'Tisn't over yet, Da. There are other ways to fill me stomach than joining the Army, other men I can throw me lot in with besides that lot of rowdies. And 'though he shan't be you, Da, I shall find a strong man I can follow yet."

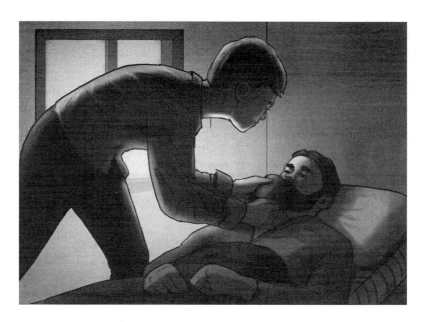

CHAPTER THREE
DOCTOR'S ORDERS

**Jemmy Martin
The Home of Dionisio Jaramillo
in Socorro, New Mexico
February 24, 1862**

Jemmy leaned against the doorsill of the adobe house and watched the sunset tint the sky pink. His family farm was far away, hundreds of miles south, just beyond the bustling town of San Antonio, Texas. He knew he couldn't see it, but knowing it was there made him stare at the southern horizon all the harder. Planting season was just beginning, and Pa, Ma and Drew would be sitting down to supper after a long day in the fields. How had Pa managed without the mules? How could he plant the fields? It made

11

his heart ache to think of his family struggling, and him not there to help.

"Water," someone behind him said, the words coming out in a shaky rasp. Jemmy turned and studied the bodies laid out in neat rows on the floor. Some twitched and writhed, their groans filling the silence. Others lay so still that Jemmy feared they had passed.

"Water," the voice said again. This time Jemmy saw that it came from a man who lay near the middle of the room.

"Coming." Jemmy picked up a bucket and ladle, then stepped over and around men until he reached the one who'd called out. He knelt and carefully helped the man raise his head a bit to drink.

"You a doctor?" the man asked after he'd drunk a dipper full.

Jemmy shook his head. "I's a packer. But I's lost my mules and my wagon got burned, so I's helping out best I kin."

"Am I going to live?" the man asked. Jemmy wondered if the man had even heard him. How would a packer have any idea if a man would live or die of his wounds? Still, what was the point of arguing?

"'Course you are," Jemmy said. "Jest lie there a spell and let your body heal up." The man nodded and relaxed back, comforted by the words. Jemmy moved throughout the darkened room, dropping to a knee whenever he found another man awake or aware enough to take a bit of water. In the corner, he found one man whose eyes and mouth were open, unblinking and unbreathing. Jemmy shivered. He set down the bucket and ladle and made his way back through the next two rooms to the back of the house.

"Doc Covey? There's another one gone," he said.

The doctor, who'd been dozing in a chair, looked up

blearily. He ran a hand over a face lined with fatigue. He still wore a blood-splattered apron, the stains having darkened since he'd dozed off. "Tell the attendants to carry him out and add him to the wagon," Doctor Covey said. "Then, why don't you lay down near the boys and rest yourself. It's been a long day."

"But, there's so many wounded." Even as Jemmy said it, he swayed on his feet.

Doctor Covey studied Jemmy. "When was the last time you slept?"

"When we first got here," Jemmy said.

Doctor Covey nodded. "But you were up again by sunrise, right? I thought as much. You've been on your feet all day. Son, if you don't get some rest, you'll end up one of those bodies on the wagon, and I'll be short another helper. So, get some rest. That's an order. And don't worry about the body. I'll tell the attendants about it." The doctor leaned forward and pushed on the arms of the chair, grunting as he rose to his feet.

Jemmy nodded and staggered back to the room full of men. In the corner near the little beehive fireplace he found Willie, the little drummer boy he'd carried in his arms on the long march from Socorro. Next to him lay the little Mexican boy who'd been brought to him the next morning. Jemmy laid his hand on the boy's forehead and felt the heat radiating from it. The boy's breathing sounded like the purr of a housecat. Jemmy stretched himself out next to the sleeping boys. He had to rest, the doc had ordered it. But he told himself he couldn't rest for very long. There were too many who needed him.

CHAPTER FOUR
A MOTHERLODE OF MEN

Cian Lochlann
South Clear Creek, Colorado Territory
Thursday, April 25, 1861

Cian stepped to the side of the dirt track when he heard the wagon gaining on him.

"Where you headed to?" the driver asked.

"Clear Creek." Cian pointed his thumb over his back, toward the jagged, snow-covered Rockies.

The driver tugged on the reins, slowing his team. "I can take you as far as Golden City. Want a ride?"

Cian didn't have to be asked twice. He scrambled into the wagon and looked up at the brilliant blue of the sky, mouthing a word of thanks. The air was so thin up here in Colorado, so pristine. If Mam and Da were up there somewhere, watching over him, surely, they could see him better here than in the sweltering Boston tenements.

"Been prospecting long?" the driver asked as he shook the reins and got the team moving again.

"How do you know I'm a prospector?" Cian asked.

The man laughed. "Everyone's a prospector. A year ago, Denver wasn't more than a few log cabins and tepees spread along the Platte River. Then, all you would-be prospectors came swarming in and wood-frame stores and saloons sprouted like May flowers after an April rain. You all are making me a rich man, keeping you supplied."

Cian nodded. "The day after I came to Denver, I picked a copy of the *Cherry Creek Rocky Mountain News* off a dusty street. I read it over so many times, I have it memorized: 'A man takes a framework of heavy timber, built like a stone boat, the bottom of which is composed of iron rasps. He hoists the framework to the top of Pike's Peak, gets on, and slides down the mountain. As he goes down, the rasps on the bottom of the framework scrape off the gold in immense shavings, which curl up onto the machine. By the time the man gets to the bottom, a ton of gold, more or less, is following him.'"

The driver laughed. "Find any of those immense shavings?"

Cian snorted and spat over the side of the wagon. "Only t'ing I found was that the *Cherry Creek Rocky Mountain News* prints more fiction than fact."

"That's a fact, alright," the driver said.

At Golden City, Cian climbed out of the merchant's wagon, thanked the driver, and began the climb up Clear Creek. His heart pounded as he gasped to take in the thin, pine-scented air. He wished Da had lived to see the gray granite crags that soared above him, so high that they never lost their snowy caps. Da had gloried in growing up in the shadow of *Carrauntoohil,* but Ireland's tallest mountain was puny next to these lofty peaks. The Rockies were beautiful, but they made for hard living, the swings in weather brutal and dangerous at this altitude.

As he neared the claim, Cian heard the rhythmic rattle of gravel on metal. He took a breath and steeled himself for the welcome he knew was not going to be warm. Cian didn't want to be here, not with these men. None of them were the leader he was searching for, nor did they care about him any more than he cared for them. Still, being with them was safer than being on his own.

The first man that Cian saw was George Nelson, who was manning the rocker. A wooden box with a metal screen bottom, the rocker was loosely set on four wooden legs. Cian watched George pour a shovel full of dirt into the rocker, then pour a cup of water over the dirt with one hand as his other hand pushed the rocker back and forth. Water and dirt flowed through the screen on the bottom, leaving just the larger stones in the rocker. Cian grinned. It looked as though George was pouring water over a baby in a cradle.

"Hoy, George! Finding anything shiny?" Cian called.

George looked up, his expression changing from suspicion to disgust. "Well, look what the cat drug in! Things down in the big city not to your liking?"

"No more chance of getting rich down there than up here, and twice as many who would have been pleased to come between me and what little I might have found. Here. Let me spell you off." Cian elbowed George aside and took over pushing the rocker.

"Ain't it the truth? Well, you did not miss anything here. One less mouth to feed, and we still durn near starved. My mother said I would never amount to much, and I guess she was right. Anyhoo, we are right glad to have you back."

"And glad to be back among friends, am I," Cian lied, knowing that George wouldn't believe him any more than he believed George. He pulled something shiny out of the rocker, bit it to test its hardness, then threw it over his shoulder. "So, how do Luther and Samuel fare these days?"

George shook his head. "None of us is getting any fatter up here, but we ain't starving, neither. I worked over this here gulch three times, and I figure it ain't good for much more. I think Samuel and Luther's claims is about played out as well. Time we pack it in and travel someplace a little more promising."

Cian nodded. "Pull up stakes if you feel the need. But don't be getting fooled into laying claim to salted land again." It was common for hucksters to fire a shotgun loaded with gold bits into the earth to "salt" it before they sold it to naive buyers. Although he never had proof, George frequently complained that his land must have been salted. He'd found some gold early on, but it had quickly petered out.

George took back the rocker, and Cian climbed to the wide ledge on which the tent stood. He found Samuel Cook hunched on a log by the fire ring, his thin face furrowed in concentration as his dark, close-set eyes scanned a sheet of newsprint. Cook looked over the top of the paper and gave Cian the wolfish smile that always made his stomach clench. Samuel Cook could be trusted to take advantage of every situation and make it play out for his own good. The trick was to convince him that it was for his own good to treat his fellow miners well.

Sam carefully folded the paper and slid it into his vest pocket. "Ah! The Prodigal Son returns! Welcome back to the land of milk and honey, Key! Glad to have our good luck charm back! Our mascot! The key to our success! Get me another cup of coffee, son. And I am *starved*. Think it time to make supper?"

Cian winced. He wasn't the key to anyone's luck. But if he'd ingratiated himself when he first arrived at camp by being a pretty fair cook by mountain man standards, he could do it again now. He picked a dented tin cup off the ground and wiped it clean with his handkerchief, then wrapped the handkerchief around the coffee pot's wire handle and lifted it from the embers. The coffee came out thin and light, telling him that this was probably the third or fourth time they'd brewed with the same beans. He handed the cup to Cook, then threw a few sticks on the ashes and blew until they caught fire. In the chuck box, Cian found a rasher of bacon wrapped in burlap, a sack of beans, and a few shriveled potatoes. Soon the bacon and potatoes sizzled in a cast iron skillet on the fire while the beans soaked for tomorrow.

"Things not go well in Denver?" Sam asked.

Cian snorted. "Couldn't find anyone who was interested in the likes of me. Called me Irish scum, they did. Threw me out on me bum."

Samuel Cook slapped Cian on the back and chuckled. "Well, they were half right. You may be Irish scum, but whether or not they know it, Irish scum is just what this world needs. Hardscrabble. Hardheaded. Tough as nails and with a temper to match. So never you fear. Those fools down in Denver might not take you, but I will. You'll be one of my first recruits."

Cian lifted one eyebrow. "Recruits for what?"

"My company, Key! We're joining the army!" Samuel pulled the paper from his vest pocket and snapped it open. "This article states that the U.S. government is so desperate to defend itself from secessionist aggression that any man who recruits twenty-five volunteers can become an officer and lead his own troops. Think of it! Me, an officer! And making sixty greenbacks a month!"

Cian winced. "And why would I want to be joining a fight I have no part in? Union, Confederate: I have no quarrel with either side."

"You've got a quarrel with an empty stomach, right? I should think you would be thrilled at the prospect of regular meals, warm clothing, and a comfortable bed, all courtesy of the U.S. Army! Who knows? By the time we get ourselves organized and signed up, the war might be over. But a contract is a contract, and I believe they'll still have to feed and clothe and shelter us for the six months we sign up for, war or no war."

"T'inkin' is believin'," Cian said with a grin.

"And I believe in my plan completely! You are my first recruit, Private Key! Sign on and be guaranteed eleven dollars a month to spend as you please!"

Cook's gaze snapped to Luther Wilson, who was scrambling down the hill towards them, his jaw jutting out defiantly, as if looking for a fight. "And here comes my second. Hey, Luther! Want to be a lieutenant in my cavalry company? Pay's fifty dollars a month."

Luther Wilson glanced up and snorted. "Sure, Sam. Why the hell not? That is fifty dollars more than I am likely to get out of this poor dirt."

"Fifty?" Cian whined. "Jaysus! Why does he get fifty and a lieutenancy when I'm offered only eleven dollars and a private's rank?"

"Ask me again when you can shave, Key. Wilson's a grown man and you are a stripling! Wet behind the ears! I might just leave you on the vine 'til you've grown a bit more."

Cian hurried to get a second cup of coffee for Wilson.

If they were going to be in a company together, they had better be on good terms. He wrinkled up his forehead, trying to think through what he'd just learned. Cavalry? Is that what Cook said? Did that mean he'd have to get on the back of an infernal horse and ride the thing?

Cook's eyes gleamed. "And I can count on George. He can be my second lieutenant. By gum, we are almost done recruiting and we have not even started."

Wilson took the coffee Cian offered and squatted down, frowning into the skillet. "We are the easy part. Your keester didn't even leave that stump," Wilson said, pointing at the log Sam was warming with his behind. But how shall you get the others? Men are spread pretty thin through these ridges and vales. You will do a good deal of walking to hit every mining camp in the district, and that is what you will have to do to recruit twenty-two more men. I say you fail."

"Fail at what? Two bucks says he succeeds. What smells so good?" George Nelson sniffed the air as he scrambled up the slope towards them.

"Potatoes and bacon," Cian said. Mam had always said that the way to a man's heart was through his stomach, and it seemed to be working. None of the three had called him a hothead or told him to get lost.

"Luther here says I cannot recruit a company," Samuel said, rubbing his hands together. "Colorado might not have gold lying around, but it has a motherlode of disillusioned young miners. I can work that seam of men more easily than any gold seam in these Rocky Mountains, and at greater profit to myself. So, tomorrow I ride into Denver..."

"And buy more food," Cian interrupted.

Samuel Cook waved his hand dismissively. "All right, then, I buy food; but while I'm doing that, I also have a printer strike off recruiting posters. Then Key here will plaster the district with them. Ya gotta earn your keep, Key. Boys, by August, we should be on our way!"

"Suppose you give me a commission! That be something to write home to Mother!" George said.

Sam Cook laughed again. "Sure, George. You can be my second lieutenant. And Cian here can be in charge of the officer's mess."

"Second Lieutenant! Boy howdy! And do I get paid, too?"

"Forty-five big ones, every month," Samuel Cook said.

"Let's eat to that!" Nelson picked a tin plate out of the dirt and wiped it clean with his elbow. Cian smiled as he spooned out the food. As long as he kept the grub warm and Cook included him in his scheming, Cian knew where his next meal was coming from. For now, that was enough. He would deal with the cavalry part later.

CHAPTER FIVE
FUNGILLO

**Jemmy Martin
The Home of Dionisio Jaramillo
Socorro, New Mexico
February 25, 1862**

Jemmy jolted awake to the scritch-scratching sound of a broom. For a moment, he thought he was back on the farm outside of San Antonio. He sat up, eager to see his Ma. Instead, the person sweeping the adobe house's packed dirt floor was a thin young man, probably no older than he was, with dark hair. Jemmy rubbed his face with his hand as he remembered that he was nowhere near his family farm.

"*Buenos dias,*" the sweeper said with a nod of his head.

Jemmy nodded back. "*Buenos dias*," he parroted.

"*¿Dormiste bien?*"

Jemmy scratched his head, making the blond hairs stand up. "Huh? No *comprehendo* you."

The man smiled and set the broom against the wall before squatting down to Jemmy's level. "I asked if you slept well."

"Oh," Jemmy said. "I did. Thank you." He looked past the man, at the dark shapes of men wrapped in blankets and sleeping all around him. A few leaned against the walls. They, too, looked asleep. Jemmy could see lines of light surrounding the door, where early morning sunshine seeped through the cracks. Dim light came through the high, mica-covered windows. "Is it morning already?"

"Nearly morning. You slept all night without twitching once. You must have been very tired." The dark-haired man stuck out his hand. "I am Fungillo Jaramillo, and this is my house. Or, actually, the house of my father, Dionisio. But I live here, too."

"Your family, are they sleeping in another room?" Jemmy asked.

Fungillo shook his head. "They are staying with my uncle. It is a little crowded here, no?"

Jemmy nodded. "It is a little crowded, yes. I'm sorry we took over your house. I know my Ma and Pa wouldn't be happy if some blue backs came waltzing into our place."

"Blue backs?" Fungillo asked.

"It's one of the things we call Union soldiers. One of the more polite things," Jemmy said, smiling a little sheepishly.

"Ah." Fungillo shrugged. "This name calling, and this house taking: I suppose they are what happens in war. We are no happier to have Texans here than you would be to have those you call blue backs."

"Then why are you serving us?" Jemmy asked.

Fungillo snorted and got back to his feet. "I am not serving you. I am here to protect the house. To make sure you don't steal our cooking pot or smash our plates."

"I'm sorry. I didn't mean to..." Jemmy began, but Fungillo cut him off.

"And to make sure our wounded get as good care as yours. We don't want our men dying of neglect." The dark-haired man started sweeping so hard that clouds of dust rose from the hard-packed floor.

Jemmy was sure the broom was doing more damage than good. "We wouldn't neglect anyone."

"Make sure you don't," Fungillo said. "Especially Arsenio Atencio. His uncle is a very important man."

Jemmy frowned. "Who?"

Fungillo jerked his chin towards the little boy who slept next to Willie. Like Willie, his hair was as black as a raven's wing, but where Willie's skin was so pale that it was almost translucent, this boy's skin was golden. Jemmy laid a gentle hand on Arsenio's forehead. It was still warm, but wasn't burning up with fever as it had been the night before.

"Aresenio Atencio. Big name for a little britches like this," Jemmy said.

"Little britches?" Fungillo's eyebrows went up questioningly.

"It's one of the things we call young'uns. And it ain't a mean or impolite thing at all," Jemmy said.

Fungillo nodded. "Blue backs. Little Britches. Before you are gone, I'm going to learn some Americano phrases, no?"

Jemmy smiled back. "Only if'n you'll teach me some Mexican ones in return. Deal?"

Fungillo smiled back. "*Es un trato*. That means, deal."

Chapter Six
Calamity

Cian Lochlann
South Clear Creek, Colorado Territory
August 19, 1861

Cian tugged on the hem of Samuel Cook's jacket. "Sam..."

"Not now, Key. Can you not see how busy I am?" Cook waved one hand distractedly, as if shooing a fly, then started sweeping both arms around in a gathering gesture. "Alright, men. To me."

"Hey, Sam. Let me call the men together. I'm the second lieutenant!" George Nelson began shouting orders that were both confusing and contradictory. "ATTENTION! LEFT FACE! FALL IN!"

"'Tis important." Cian winced at the whine in his voice. Time was running short. If he was ever going to confess to Sam that he couldn't ride, it had to be now.

Eighty-three men had joined Cook, Nelson, and Wilson after Cian plastered every barn and building in the entire mining district with recruiting posters. Mostly down-and-out miners and frontiersmen, they were a rowdy bunch, always spoiling for a fight, and they didn't care whether it was against the Confederates or someone else. The company included six more Irishmen besides Cian, four Scots, two Germans who could barely speak English, and a Welshman with an accent so thick that Cian would've sworn he was speaking a different language entirely. Once they were sworn in, they would be a company of cavalry. Samuel Cook would be their captain.

Cian didn't like the looks of these men. He was definitely the smallest of the group, and probably the youngest as well. If he didn't find a way to fit in, he might end up being the brunt of all their practical jokes and a slave to every one of them. His gaze rested on one man who leaned against a post, a little apart from the rest. He, too, had a slight build, but what surprised Cian more than anything was that he was reading a book! It had been a long time since Cian had seen anyone do that.

"Alright, men," Sam began when the men stopped elbowing one another, "Tomorrow we ride out, bound for Fort Leavenworth. I just got a letter from Senator Lane, and it says he shall accept us into the Kansas Brigade when we get there."

"Good man, Jim Lane. Worthy to be both Senator and General. I know. I served with him in the Mexican-American," one man shouted, but Cook silenced him with a wave of his hand.

"You each paid me five dollars, for expenses incurred

before we reach post. That'll keep us in beans and bacon for quite some time."

"What? No oysters and caviar? You can do better than beans," one of the men interrupted, to the loud guffaws of the others. Cook glared at them and they settled down.

"The faster we get to Leavenworth, the faster we get on the Union payroll. That means salary, sure, but also steady rations, new uniforms and equipment, and new mounts. The old, broken-down nags we were able to buy here will be replaced."

The men roared with approval, but Cian felt his heart sink. He tugged at Cook's jacket again. "Sam?"

"So, get some rest," Cook continued, "and say your goodbyes. We shall stop in Denver for lunch before heading east." He turned toward Cian, but George Nelson got between the two.

"May I dismiss the men? I'm your Second Lieutenant. Let me do it! Please, Sam."

Cian looked at the crowd, which was already dispersing. They didn't need George to tell them the lecture was over, but Sam gave a cursory nod and George bellowed "BREAK RANKS, MARCH!" at the retreating backs. Only George Nelson and Luther Wilson remained.

"Now what, Key? What can be so important that you have to interrupt my first address to the troops?" Sam's voice was gravelly with impatience.

"I am thinking now that I shan't be going with you tomorrow." The words felt like sandpaper in Cian's mouth. He swallowed twice, then looked up at Sam's face. He didn't see the anger he'd expected, but confusion and a bit of humor.

"You mean to say you have found a girl you cannot leave behind?"

Cian felt his cheeks flush. "No, Sam. Nothing like that."

"Then what?" Sam pulled his watch out of his vest pocket and examined the time. Clearly, he wasn't in the mood to beat around the bush.

"I cannot ride," Cian said in a voice so tiny that he couldn't hear it over his own pulse, pounding in his ears.

"You cannot what?"

"RIDE," Cian said. "I never learned to sit a horse."

Samuel Cook let out a burst of laughter. "Then why in blazes did you join a cavalry company?"

Cian shrugged, unsure what to say. "For you, Sam. To stay with you. I thought I would learn, but..."

"Well, we are damn short of time to teach you now."

Luther cackled with glee as he slapped his hand on Cian's shoulder. "You got enough to worry about, Sam. I'll take care of this. C'mon, George, get Calamity saddled up."

As Luther manhandled him towards the horse pasture, Cian protested that he wasn't ready to ride, especially a horse with the unlucky name of Calamity, but all his arguing accomplished was drawing a crowd. By the time George led the little roan mare to the fence, the majority of the company was making wagers on how long he'd stay in the saddle.

"This here is Calamity. Now, ain't she a sweet little thing?" Luther reached over the fence and stroked a pony's nose. Relieved, Cian reached over too. Calamity wasn't a horse at all, but a petite little pony. Surely, she couldn't be as bad as her name. Perhaps she was one of those beasts who was called something that was opposite of her nature as some sort of a joke. Back in Boston he'd known a woman with a teeny, toothless terrier named Killer.

At the touch of Cian's hand, Calamity's velvety nostrils flared. She pulled back her head and nuzzled his hand gently with her big, soft lips. Her teeth champed on the bit, but it wasn't a threatening, grinding sound. Cian looked to Luther, his face full of hope. "You are not trying to hornswoggle me, are you, Luther? We are chums, aren't we now?"

"'Course we are. Calamity's a bit skittish, but you need not worry. Just get on her back and hang on. Before you know it, you'll be riding her like an old pro."

Luther helped Cian climb the fence. Cian jammed his hat down hard on his head, spit on the palms of his hands, then took hold of the reins just like Luther told him to. He stuck one foot in the stirrup, then swung his other leg over the pony.

For a moment the pony stood still and Cian relaxed. He looked up and smiled at the men who leaned against the fence and leered back at him.

And then all hell broke loose. Calamity went rigid. She jerked her head down, hunched her back, and threw out her back legs, bucking wildly.

A throaty roar went up from the men along the fence.

Cian's left hand pulled the reins over his head. He clutched at the saddle horn with his other hand, leaning forward. Just as he caught his balance, Calamity threw back her head. Her neck slammed into Cian's face, sending his hat flying. Color bloomed in Cian's vision. His face exploded in pain. He dropped the reins and palmed his nose. Blood spurted out from between his fingers.

Calamity spun. Cian felt himself slipping sideways. He grabbed a handful of mane and leaned away from the ground. Just as he managed to reseat himself, Calamity bolted. Cian leaned over her neck and for a moment the two of them galloped across the pasture. Then the pony pulled up short and Cian flew over her shoulder. He struck the ground and tumbled head over heels. When he finally stopped moving, he heard men loudly guffawing.

Cian squeezed his eyes shut, fighting back tears that

were a confusion of outrage and pain. His whole body and soul ached. He wanted to melt into the ground so he wouldn't have to face the men's wicked grins. He wanted to punch both Luther and George square in the face so that their noses hurt as badly as his did. He hated them all, every man in the whole of Cook's troop.

A shadow covered his face, so Cian opened one eye a bit and found George standing over him, a goofy grin on his face. "If that don't beat all, Key! You stayed on a full count of ten! We are rich!"

Cian groaned. "Jaysus, Mary and Joseph! When I get back on my feet, you and Luther are dead men."

"Do not get all wrathy on me, Key. It were nothing but a bit of hijinks." George grabbed Cian by the armpits and hauled him to his feet. "Luther and me knew you could do it. You got that stubborn Irish streak what makes you hang on like a pit bull with lockjaw. That is why we bet on you."

"I could have been killed." Cian's legs shook so much he thought he might tumble back into the dirt. He ached all over. He gingerly touched his nose, sure it was broken.

"But you survived, and we are all a good deal richer for the wear," Luther said as he walked up. He held out a fat roll of bills. "Here is your share, George, and here is yours, Key."

Cian slapped Luther's hand away. "You lied to me, Luther! You said Calamity was a good horse!"

Luther shook his head. "I never said the like. I said she was a sweet little thing, and that she is, leastwise till you mount her. And I said she was a little skittish, and that is true in spades. But I also promised that if you hung on, you would soon be riding her like an old pro, and that is what you are. Pros get paid for their work, and here is your pay. Go ahead: Take it. It will help tide you over once we are gone."

"Well now, I do not know about the pro part, but I certainly feel old. Aigh! My aching back!" Cian snatched the wad of bills from Luther's hand and stuffed them in his pocket. "But about this 'once you are gone?' You think I am going to let you leave without me? You have got another think coming. Now, find me something with a little less spitfire than that Calamity and teach me to ride, like you promised, Sam."

"I can help."

Cian spun around and found the man who had been reading standing behind him. The man took a step toward him and held out his hand.

"I taught my younger brothers and sisters to ride. I could teach you. I am Edward Pillier, by the way, of Burlington, Colorado, but my friends call me E.D."

Cian narrowed his eyes. He looked up and down E.D.'s lanky frame. "And why would you be offering me this help?"

E.D. shrugged. "Seems like you need it."

"You expecting a part of this money I just earned?"

"Not at all." E.D. spread his hands, palms skyward. "You earned it; you keep it. It just looked to me like you were going to need some help if you were going to ride with the Company, and right now, I've got nothing better to do than to be helpful."

Cian studied E.D. up and down, looking for the trick or the trap. No one offered something for free. E.D. continued to gaze at Cian. His eyes didn't flicker away like someone who was trying to con him. Finally, Cian decided that this E.D. fellow was honest. He turned and glared at Luther and George, hoping that they could see the defiance in his eyes. "Then come on, Edward Pillier of Burlington, Colorado. We've a bit of work to do."

CHAPTER SEVEN
EL BURRO SABE

Jemmy Martin
The Home of Dionisio Jaramillo
Socorro, New Mexico
February 25, 1862

"Arsenio Atencio. Arsenio Atencio. Arsenio Atencio." As he rolled strips of cotton torn from a sheet, Jemmy repeated the name of the boy who lay next to Willie, letting the syllables roll off his tongue as if they were the words to a song. Arsenio had been burning up with fever, and his breath had come and gone in wheezing gasps when his brother had carried him in. Now, he lay still, his breathing far less labored.

The hair on the back of Jemmy's neck rose as he remembered seeing what he'd thought was the ghost of the young man he had killed at the Battle of Valverde walking toward the hospital with Arsenio in his arms. But the man, whom Fungillo had explained was named Raul, was no ghost. He'd thanked Jemmy for being a bad shot and asked him to take care of Arsenio, which Jemmy had happily done, grateful for a chance to atone for having shot at Raul, even if he did miss him.

"Arsenio Atencio. Arsenio Atencio. Arsenio Atencio," he repeated. Someone cleared his throat at the doorway and Jemmy looked up to find Fungillo and Raul standing there. "The doctor, he wants to know if you are finished rolling the bandages. And Raul wants to know why you are saying his brother's name over and over," Fungillo Jaramillo said.

Jemmy held up the roll he was working on. "I've done ten. Got two or three more to do after I finish this one. And the name sounds purty," Jemmy said with a shrug. "Like what old Macdonald said."

Fungillo laughed and said something to Raul that Jemmy could not understand. Raul scowled and growled a response before Fungillo turned back to Jemmy. "I will let the doctor know when you are finished. We will use them to rebandage the wounds that have bled through their old bandages. And you are not using Arsenio's name to cast a spell or something, no? And what is it that this old Macdonald said?"

"E-I-E-I-O," Jemmy said.

"Ah," said Fungillo. "Now, here is something for you to say: Ah, Eh, EEE, Oh, OOO. *El burro sabe mas que tu.*" Fungillo repeated it three times, and then Jemmy said it back. Raul crossed his arms over his chest and chuckled.

"And what does that mean?" Jemmy said, when Fungillo had nodded in approval.

"It is the vowels, A, E, I, O, U, and then 'a burro knows more than you do.'"

Jemmy nodded. "I had two mules that were both smarter than me, so I believe it. I think I like saying Arsenio Atencio better. Arsenio Atencio. Arsenio Atencio. Oh look! He's awake."

Jemmy jerked his chin toward the boy, whose dark brown eyes were staring in horror at him. Immediately, Raul crossed the room and gathered his brother in his arms. He spoke in rapid Spanish, which to Jemmy's ears, meant no more than what Old Macdonald's vowels did, but even if he couldn't understand the words, he could hear the tenderness in the tone.

"What're they saying?" Jemmy asked Fungillo.

"The little one, he heard his brother ask me if you were casting an evil spell on him. Raul, he says no, that you can be trusted. You are so impressed by his strong and noble name that you say it over and over."

A wave of gratitude warmed Jemmy's heart. He stood and Raul and Arsenio gave a low bow. "Will you tell the strong and noble *Señor* Arsenio Atencio and his worthy brother that I am at their service until Arsenio recovers his health?" As the three locals talked, Jemmy sat back down and rolled the remaining strips of sheet. He tucked one into his pocket, then picked up the basket which held the others. "Fungillo, I'm going to let Doc Covey know I'm done. You think you could find me a thin wood shingle? I gots me an idea for something to keep Arsenio and Willie busy."

Fungillo frowned, thinking for a moment, then nodded. "I think I could do that."

CHAPTER EIGHT
KANSAS OR BUST

Cian Lochlann
Denver, Colorado Territory
August 20, 1861

Samuel Cook and his ragtag troop turned onto Larimer Street in Denver and found the Territorial Governor, William Gilpin, waiting for them. Cian was so stiff and saddle sore that he didn't hear any of the Governor's welcoming speech. He slumped on Henrietta's back, dozing. The docile little hinny, a cross between a stallion and a donkey mare, let him do just that. All day, the little hinny, who was called a tobiano because she had spots and looked like a miniature version of her brown and white paint father but with the short mane and tail of a donkey, had stoically tolerated his slumping and double-bouncing as she'd trotted. More than once Luther or George had reminded him that he had no control over his mount if he held his reins way up near his shoulders. Luckily for him, Henrietta had followed the others, ignoring Cian.

Eventually, Cian learned that riding was more about balance than grip. He stopped clothespinning Henrietta's back with his legs and relaxed, but by that point he was already awfully sore.

Cian jerked awake when someone slapped his arm. "The speechifying is over. Time for lunch, if you can bear to be parted with that brevet horse of yours," George said teasingly.

"Brevet?" Cian asked.

George nodded. "When a soldier does well in battle, he gets a brevet: a promotion to a higher rank. That hinny of yours deserves a brevet, carrying that sack of potatoes all day."

"I never saw anyone jerk and hulk in a saddle as much as you do," Luther added.

Cian patted Henrietta's brown and white spotted neck. "She deserves a promotion for keeping me in the saddle all day. She is as noble a steed as any in the troop, even if she is small."

George laughed. "Fer you, small is good. Makes yer fall all the shorter."

Almost as soon as he slid out of the saddle, Cian's knees buckled under him. He clung desperately to the saddle horn. This, too, Henrietta endured with little more than a little nicker as she shifted to steady herself.

"Where's Cook got himself off to?" he asked when he'd finally found his land legs again.

Luther shrugged. "He and the Governor are out peacocking around. They're planning on eating in the hoity-toity Sutherland House. Us regular folks have to make do with regular victuals. Here." He pulled a chunk of beef jerky out of his saddle bag and handed it to Cian, who took it gratefully. They led their mounts to a water trough and let them drink while they shared a bushel of apples and a paper packet of crackers that one of the men bought at E. Karczewsky & Co's store. They were still milling about when Samuel Cook strode back, waving his arms and looking harried.

"Alright, men. To me."

"ATTEN-SHUN!" George shouted.

Samuel Cook let out an exasperated sigh. "Thank you, Lieutenant Nelson. Men, I come to you with a proposition that Governor Gilpin made to me on your behalf. I know that you thought we were Kansas bound, and Kansas bound we shall be if you but say the word, but the Governor of our fine territory beseeches us to consider staying here and protecting what is ours."

"What are you yammering on about? Speak in plain English, Cook!" one of the men in the crowd shouted.

As the rest murmured amongst themselves, Samuel held out his hands and waited for the men to quiet. "What I mean is this: Governor Gilpin worries about the safety of the Colorado Territory. We have enemies within. The secessionists have many sympathizers who would wrest the territory from the Union and hand her and her resources to the rebellious South. Furthermore, word has it that a Henry H. Sibley, recently of the United States Army, left his post this spring and is now recruiting an army in Texas, the purpose of which is to invade first New Mexico Territory, then our own dear Territory of Colorado before moving on and seizing California, its gold fields and ports, for the Confederacy."

Low, angry muttering rose among the men. Samuel

put his hand out to still them. "I see the news has affected you as it affected me. To see our own dear Colorado attacked by those deplorable secessionists is more than either I or your Governor can abide. Governor Gilpin has been asked by Lincoln himself to protect the territory at all costs, and he intends to do just that. To that aim, the governor has asked us to stay here in Denver and gallantly protect the territory. He promises that we will be well mounted, well-armed, and well equipped. Only but say the word, men, and our journey to find glory is at an end. Say the word, and we shall remain here and become Company F of the First Regiment of Colorado Volunteers."

Cian crossed his arms over his chest. "What's in it for you, Captain Cook? Did the Governor promise you an extra bounty for bringing in a company?"

"In it for me? Can a man not rise to defend his country without being accused of lining his own pockets?" Samuel Cook placed his hands on his chest and affected surprised innocence. He wasn't fooling Cian, who'd known him long enough to know that he always had an ulterior motive.

"I shall do it, provided pay and facilities stay the same," Luther Wilson said.

"They shall," Cook assured him. The men gave a mighty cheer. Cook silenced them with a gesture. "Then we have agreed. Mount up, men, and we shall proceed to our new quarters on Ferry Street and elect our officers."

"Elect? But I am second lieutenant already, Sam, ain't I? You ain't going to take that from me." George slid into his saddle, then remembering himself, bellowed at the men. "MOUNT UP! HEAD 'EM UP AND MOVE 'EM OUT!"

Cian untied Henrietta's lead rope from the saddle horn and began walking her behind the others. He was glad that they were staying in Colorado. He hadn't wanted to ride all the way to Kansas. Heck, he didn't even want to ride all the way to their new quarters. But his sixth sense was telling him that not all was on the up and up with Samuel Cook's little deal with Governor Gilpin.

CHAPTER NINE
LITTLE COMPADRES

**Jemmy Martin
The Home of Dionisio Jaramillo
Socorro, New Mexico
February 25, 1862**

Arsenio and Willie were sitting side by side, their shoulders touching when Jemmy walked into the room carrying two earthenware bowls of soup. They were so intent on whatever was on the ground between the two of them that they didn't look up. "Who's hungry? *Hambriento*?" he asked, hefting the bowls and hoping he said the word right. Arsenio's head snapped up and he nodded.

"What'cha got there?" Jemmy asked. He handed Arsenio a bowl, then knelt and spooned some stew into

Willie's mouth. With his one arm in a sling, the drummer boy had a hard time holding a bowl and eating from it.

"A dice," Willie said. He held out the little white square in his hand for Jemmy to see. "That soldier over there, he gave it to us."

Jemmy looked in the direction of Willie's pointed finger and saw a man leaning against the wall. Although his head was wrapped in cloth and one arm was bound to his side, the soldier smiled back. Jemmy nodded at him, grateful to find kindness in the midst of war.

"Nice," Jemmy said. "But it's two dice, one die. What're you doing with that die? Playing a game?"

Willie shook his head. "Learning our numbers. Watch."

He rolled the die out of his palm and it rattled between the two boys. "*Dos!*" Arsenio said, pointing at the two black spots.

"*Dos*," Willie repeated. "That means 'two.' Same as '*deux*.'"

"Dew?" Jemmy asked.

"It's French," Willie said. "I'm from Lou'sianna, 'member?"

Jemmy's eyebrows flew up. "You know French?"

"Some," Willie said. "And now some Spanish. That's what the Mexicans here speak. Not Mexican. Did you know that?"

"Two," Arsenio said, pointing at the die. "Two. *Deux*. *Dos*."

"*Bonne*! *Bueno*! An' I can eat this all by myself," Willie said, reaching for the bowl.

"You sure?" Jemmy asked.

"If I need help, my *compadre* here will help me," Willie said. Jemmy handed over the bowl, gave each boy's hair a tousle, then went back to get more bowls of stew.

Some men, like Arsenio, would be able to feed themselves. Others, like Willie, would need help.

He was washing up when Fungillo walked into the courtyard carrying something wrapped up in a red neckerchief. "Don't you chip those bowls," Fungillo said with a frown. "They belonged to my great-grandmother."

"Really?" Jemmy asked.

"Not really," Fungillo answered, his frown exploding into an outsized grin. "I am, what you call it? Pulling your leg?"

Jemmy grinned back. "How would I know? A *burro sabe mas que me*, remember? What you got in that cloth?"

Fungillo untied the knot and the neckerchief's corners fell back, exposing two wooden tops. "You wanted that shingle to make something for *los compadres*, to keep them busy. I cannot let a Texan get all the gratitude. So, I brought these. Your little drummer boy may not be able to spin this, but Arsenio, he can do it for him. How are they doing, those two?"

Jemmy nodded his head appreciatively at the tops. "They're healing up just fine. Getting along fine, too. If we could get the generals and presidents and what not to talk like those two, this war'd be over and we'd all be home by now."

Fungillo placed a hand on Jemmy's shoulder. "I used to wish you would go home for my sake, *compadre*. Now, I wish you could go home, for yours." The two looked at each other, brown eyes into blue. Jemmy wanted to say something deep and appreciative, but his mouth couldn't find words—in any language—to express how his heart swelled in his chest. Finally, he looked away.

"Let's go see what our little *compadres* think of your gift," he said.

"Ooh" and "Aah" are the same in English, Spanish and

French, and both boys made the sounds of appreciation and delight. Arsenio set his own top to spinning, then Willie's, but Willie's was the first to tip onto its side and roll to a stop. Arsenio cheered and pumped his fist in the air.

"That boy! He is just like his brother, Raul. To him, everything is a contest to be won," Fungillo said with a snort of laughter.

Jemmy shook his head. "Sometimes, it's better to fail than to succeed."

"Like when?" Fungillo asked, still laughing.

"Like when you're aiming a shotgun at someone. I'm glad I missed."

Fungillo's smile fell away, and he soberly studied Jemmy's face for a moment. "I will tell Arsenio to let the little *Americano* win sometimes. He, too, needs to learn to lose graciously." He bent down and spoke to Arsenio in Spanish, then threw back his head and laughed at the boy's reply before coming back to his feet at addressing Jemmy.

"Aresenio says he will try to be fair with how he spins the tops, but already he is on to another challenge. He bets you he will be well enough to go home before you leave Socorro."

"Tell him I hope he wins that bet," Jemmy said. "And tell him, when I do go, I hope that I go home, too." He would have said more, but the lump in his throat had grown so big that he had to squeeze his eyes shut to keep the tears from spilling out. Jemmy went to the door and leaned against the sill, looking south, towards Texas, his family farm, and all his hopes.

CHAPTER TEN
STAYING PUT

Cian Lochlann
Denver, Colorado Territory
Tuesday, October 22, 1861

Cian threw himself down on his cot. "This soldiering life is not what I expected."

"I thought all you wanted was to get fed and have a roof over your head," George Nelson said.

Cian groaned and threw an arm over his eyes. In the two months since Samuel Cook's gang had become Company F of the 1st Colorado Volunteers, they'd moved from quarters in private houses on Ferry Street to a hotel, named the Old Buffalo House that sat a little ways out of town. Cian's navel wasn't so friendly with his spine, but as his belly expanded, so had his expectations. "All we do is drill, drill, and drill some more. When we're not drilling, we're confined to quarters. I should have joined Samuel Logan's Company when I had the chance. At least they've seen some action."

In late August, Captain Logan's Company B had stormed the Criterion, a notorious secessionist saloon, with bayonets fixed on the ends of their rifles. They'd confiscated weapons and ammunition and chased the rebels out of town. Now they patrolled every evening while civilians lined the streets and cheered. It was like a parade every day.

"Samuel Logan is a bully." Nelson stood at attention, as if giving a report. "Do not forget that Company B has petitioned the Governor to remove him. They say, and I quote from the official complaint, which I have read with my own eyes, that his 'overbearance and tyranny have become intolerable.'"

Cian shrugged. "He's got the same drooping mustache and strong, broad shoulders as me Da. Was even a blacksmith like me Da. And he's a Mexican American War Veteran. And anyways, you can't read, so how would you be reading an official complaint?"

George's shoulders slumped. "I admits it. Someone else read it aloud and I rememorized it. But whether or not I read it, we all know Logan's got nothing on our Sam. Anyhoo, don't see what you got to complain about. At least you wasn't demoted like me."

Cian felt a stab of sympathy for George. "W.F. Marshall won the election for first lieutenant fair and square. First Sergeant 'tis a better fit for your talents, anyway. Sergeants get to yell at the men more often."

Nelson brightened. "I do like to boss men around! And my mother said I would never amount to much! Still,

I wish I still got those forty-five dollars a month instead of the seventeen I get now."

"Seeing as 'tis in Gilpin scrip, does it really matter what they say 'tis worth?" George couldn't argue with that. Governor Gilpin had printed $355,000 in U.S. Treasury notes, now called Gilpin scrip, to feed and house the troops. However, rumors had begun to circulate that Gilpin had no authority to print the notes, and the government was not going to back them. Many local merchants wouldn't accept them.

Cian stood up. George stepped between him and the door. "Now wait a minute, Key. You may not cotton to Army life no more, but you're not planning on absquatulating, are you? You can't desert on my watch. I am the sergeant, remember, and I order you to..." But Cian didn't stay to hear George's orders. He brushed by George, clattered down the steps, and stepped into the night. E.D. was on picket duty near the road. Talking with E.D. always settled him down.

The crisp fall air, redolent with the smoke of evening fires, smelled warm and comforting. Overhead, a thousand stars glistened. In the east, Cian could see the glow of a moon just past full that was going to rise soon. He spied a point of red light near the Buffalo House's corral. E.D. didn't smoke. He must have company. Cian wrapped his arms around himself and wished that he'd grabbed his coat on the way out the door. Although it was warm Indian Summer, up here in this high country the temperature plummeted once the sun set.

"Halt! Who goes there?" The voice wasn't E.D.'s, but it was familiar.

"Hoy, Luther. 'Tis just me, Cian."

"What are you doing out here?" The growl in Luther Wilson's voice made it clear that Cian wasn't welcome.

Even when they were still up at the claim, Luther had not been particularly friendly. Now that he was a second lieutenant, he'd taken on airs.

"I'm bored. Thought I might talk with E.D.," Cian answered.

"You got a pass? You know we are obliged to remain in quarters without one."

Cian shrugged, a movement Luther was unlikely to see in the dark.

Luther continued: "You should remain in quarters unless on official business. We have had collisions between our men and town secesh."

"And you are posted out here to stop us from getting into brawls with Southern sympathizers?" Cian asked defensively.

"More'n that. Captain Cook is in town. He instructed me to keep the company in quarters until he returned." Luther's voice dropped as if he were sharing some great secret. "Besides, scuttlebutt is that a force of Texans may be headed our way. We are here to bar them from the road into town."

"That so? And how are just you and E.D. planning to hold off a whole force of Texans?" Cian asked the question defiantly. He was so bored that he was itching for a fight. It didn't matter who it was with. Secesh, Texan, surly second lieutenant: they would all go down just as hard under Cian's frustrated fists. He was rolling up his sleeves when E.D. whirled around and pointed his rifle into the darkness beyond.

"Halt! Who goes there?" Luther called out again.

This time there was no answer.

"'Tis nobody," Cian said.

"Shhhh," E.D. said.

Cian closed his mouth and listened for a moment.

Then he heard what the other two were hearing. The shuffle of many feet. The stealthy sound of bodies bumping into bodies in the darkness. Cian peered hard, wishing that the moon had broken the eastern horizon and made the scene clear to him. He could barely make out the inky hulk that must have been a hundred men. He felt his blood run cold.

Luther Wilson snapped into action. "Private Lochlann, go back to Buffalo House and tell Sergeant Nelson to rally the troops. Send a messenger into town to let Colonel Slough know that we have uncovered the enemy and will be engaging him presently. Then get your rifle and report back to me."

Cian ran back to Buffalo House so quickly that when he got there, he didn't have wind left to speak. After a ridiculous game of pantomime, he convinced George to rally the troops and send an orderly galloping into town. Cian grabbed his rifle and raced back to the picket post.

The blackness was larger now, a shuffling, snorting menace looming ever closer. Wilson paced, cursing under his breath. "Where is that dad-burned Sergeant? Where are the troops?"

"George is mustering them as fast as he can," Cian gasped.

Luther cut him off with a hiss and a slash of the hand. "Not fast enough!" he whispered. "We will be overrun before he comes." Luther stiffened. He extended himself to his full height, standing tall and straight against the starlight. "Men, although it is just us three against the hordes of demon rebels out there, we shall make a valiant stand. We shall move around, firing from a new spot each time. Perhaps they will think we are greater in number than we are, and they will take fright and run. If not, when Sergeant Nelson and the men finally arrive, they will see our shattered bodies and know that we died heroes. Be ready on the count of three."

Cian swallowed the sand in his throat. He pulled a cartridge from the pouch on his belt, tore it open with his teeth, and poured the powder down the barrel of his rifle, then dropped in a minie ball.

"One," Luther whispered hoarsely.

Cian's hands shook so violently that he struggled to pull the ramrod from its holder and jam it down the gun barrel to pack the ball and powder down. It rattled like a saber as he placed it back in its mount. He pulled back the hammer and placed a cap from the cap box onto the rifle cone.

"Two," said Luther.

Cian checked to make sure the hammer was back all the way, then he brought the rifle to his shoulder and aimed down its barrel. At what? All was dusky darkness.

"Three!" Luther shouted. Cian and E.D. squeezed their triggers and the air exploded into bangs. The attackers bellowed, crashing about as they sought safety. As Cian and E.D. reloaded, Luther hopped about, firing his pistol. After five shots, he hunkered down and reloaded, following the same multistep process that Cian and the guard followed. They were still running hither and yon, loading and shooting sporadically when a half dozen officers cantered out of the town and pulled up near them.

"Cease fire!" one of the officers shouted in a ringing voice. Cian, who'd just reloaded, let go one more round for good measure. "I said, cease your fire! Captain! Report!"

Luther Wilson snapped into a sharp salute just as the moon rose, illuminating his face. "Second Lieutenant Luther Wilson, Company F reporting, sir! Captain Cook is on leave in town at present, and left me in command. We have the enemy pinned down. Or he has retreated. We are not sure. It is... dark... sir."

"I can see that," the man said with a derisive snort. "You there: Private. Go scout the enemy position. Report back as soon as you understand their numbers."

"Me, sir?" E.D. swallowed so hard that Cian could hear it, then slipped reluctantly away.

Cian squinted, trying to identify the man who was giving the commands. He sat astride a large gray horse, a giant of a man with a deep, resonant voice that commanded respect. The moon rose behind him, shadowing his face. Cian could not make out his features, but the man had a round head and his face was encircled with wispy sideburns that shone in the moonlight.

"Hup! Hup! Hup! Hup! Aaaaand, halt! Lookie, Luther! Men, the boys are here! We marched double time!" As most of a company of men bumped into each other in their abrupt attempt to halt, Cian heard triumph in George Nelson's voice, even if he couldn't see the smile on his face.

"What took you so long?" Luther snapped.

"Shucks, Luther! You did not want us going into our first conflict looking ragged, now did ya? I had to make sure everyone passed inspection afore we marched off to face the enemy."

Luther and George might have gotten into a fist fight had not the large man on the horse commanded silence. For a long moment everyone stood still, waiting, hope-filled, for E.D.'s return.

"Well?" the man on the gray horse boomed when E.D. had saluted. "How many Grey Backs did you see?"

"None, sir," E.D. said in a little peep of a voice.

Luther Wilson swayed on his feet. His voice sounded stricken. "No Confederates sneaking up on us? Were they Comanches, then?"

"No, sir," the picket peeped.

"What, pray tell, were you firing at?" the man on the horse asked in a voice that could shake the heavens.

"Beeves," E.D. said.

"Beeves?" The man's voice rose as he stood in the saddle, looking like an Old Testament prophet pronouncing doom. "You mean to tell me that the host of Texans you fancied you were repulsing was actually a drove of stock?"

"Yes, sir. Black Angus. We got two of them."

"That means feasting tomorrow!" George crowed gleefully.

"We shall see about that," the man boomed. "Perkins: Get some orderlies out here to butcher the dead beeves. You three: For your unwarranted war against cows, I want you confined to the guardhouse for three days. The rest of you are dismissed. Come on, men." The mounted men turned and trotted back toward town. As he watched them disappear into the darkness, Cian's fingers tightened into fists, then flexed open as his emotions swung from anger at being punished to a yearning for this man's leadership.

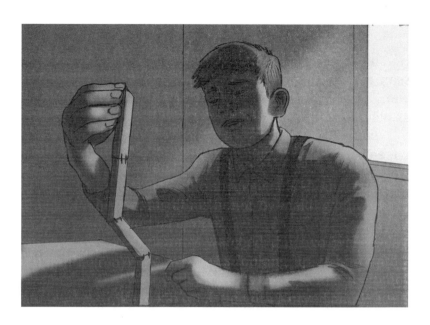

CHAPTER ELEVEN
MOVING OUT

Jemmy Martin
The Home of Dionisio Jaramillo
Socorro, New Mexico
February 26, 1862

Jemmy smiled down at the two *compadres*, who were babbling to each other as they moved sticks about on the hard packed earth floor. "Making patterns?" he asked.

Willie looked up. His eyes sparkled. "No, Jemmy. We's luchandoing."

Arsenio nodded. "*Luchando contra el Turco.*" He picked up one of the sticks and knocked it against another, making an explosive sound as he did so.

Jemmy nodded. The two boys were battling the Turks.

He shook his head. Witnessing a real battle might have scared Willie, but not enough to make him stop playing at war. "Here. I made these for you. Maybe they're not as fun as playing soldier, but I thought you'd enjoy 'em."

Jemmy reached into his pocket and brought out what appeared to be six wooden squares bound together with strips of cloth. He held one of the squares between his thumb and middle finger, and the rest dropped down until they hung in a straight line.

Willie reached out to grab the blocks. "Those can be pontoon bridges, as we cross Peloponnesus."

"Cross the what?" Jemmy said. "Maybe they kin do that. Look what else they kin do." Jemmy turned over the square in his hand, and it seemed to tumble down the others, clacking away until it reached the bottom. Arsenio burst into a string of words so quick that Jemmy couldn't make them out, but could tell meant the boy was amazed.

"Here," Jemmy bundled up the squares and handed them to Willie. "*Uno por tu, y uno por tu.*" He pulled a second bundle and gave it to Arsenio. The air was filled with the clacking of wood and the chatter of the two boys.

Fungillo peered through the door, obviously attracted by the sound. "*Bueno*, my friend. These, I take it, are what you needed the shingle for?"

"*Si, mi amigo,*" Jemmy answered back. "They ain't as fancy as yer tops, but they'll keep 'em busy awhile. My Pa used to make these fer my brother and me. Called them Jacob's ladders."

Fungillo nodded. "Same as we call them. *Escalera de Jacob.*"

Jemmy wiggled his fingers as his hand rose through the air. "You *scale* up a ladder. Es-*scale-e*ra. I think I kin remember that." They smiled down at the two younger boys, pleased with each other's company. Although it had only been a few days, Jemmy had grown attached to Aresenio and Fungillo. Fungillo was honest and hardworking, not at all shiftless and lazy like the people his Pa had told him lived in New Mexico. He couldn't wait to get home and tell his Pa how wrong he'd been.

Doc Covey walked through the door. He studied Willie and Arsenio, who were so busy that they didn't notice the doctor's arrival. "Looks like they're both healing up nicely. That's good; two less for us to worry about when we move out tomorrow."

Jemmy's head snapped to attention. "We's movin'? Tomorrow?"

"That's right. General Sibley's decided that those who are able bodied have recovered from the battle and the march, so it's time to continue north."

"But, what about these men?" Jemmy gestured about the room at the men who lay about on blankets. A few had died in the past few days. Others looked like they would die soon. None looked like they had recovered from the battle or the march to Socorro. Fungillo grabbed up the bucket of water and the ladle and began moving among the men while Jemmy followed the Doctor into the next room.

"These men are not part of the able-bodied, obviously," Doc Covey said. "They're not going anywhere soon."

"We're staying put, right? To care for them?" Jemmy felt a flutter of hope. It died out as the doctor shook his head.

"The General wants me to move on when the troops march out, and so I will. The walking wounded—those who can function to some degree but are not able to fight—will have to take over our duties. The men we leave here will either recover and join us, or they won't. Sooner or later, they'll either be buried or they'll leave of their own accord."

Jemmy's stomach flopped like a fish on the shore. "How about I stay here and look after these men? I don't got no wagon to pack, no mules to drive. No point in me going on."

Doc Covey stared at Jemmy over the top of his half-moon glasses. "Are you injured? Can you still shoulder a firearm?"

"Well, no. I mean, yes." Jemmy threw up his hands in frustration. "Doc, I don't intend to shoot no one, even if I *can* shoulder a firearm. I ain't no soldier."

"But you're able bodied. All able-bodied men are to continue north. General's orders. I won't make you fight, of course; I need you in the medical corps. Be ready to move out at dawn." Jemmy watched Doc Covey step back through the doorway, giving orders with a jab of his finger as he passed through the next room. He squeezed his eyes shut and thought about what leaving Socorro would mean: Another long march, another series of encampments along the Rio Grande, and, sooner or later, another battle.

Jemmy turned back and looked at the two young boys who were still turning the top squares of their *escaleros.* Was that the word for them? Try as he might, Jemmy couldn't get these new words to form right on his tongue. Willie, though, seemed to be having no trouble talking with Arsenio.

"Ready? One. *Dos. Trois,*" Willie shouted. The two boys laughed as they flipped their hands and cheered as their blocks raced to the bottom. How could Jemmy uproot Willie from this place where he had found someone to laugh with? What would be the point of exposing him to more danger? Although it broke his heart to leave Willie behind, Jemmy knew it was the right thing to do.

He cleared his throat, and when Fungillo looked up at the sound, Jemmy jerked his head, indicating the door. Fungillo nodded, set down the bucket, and went outside. A moment later, Jemmy followed him.

"What is it, my friend? You looked worried," Fungillo said.

Jemmy leaned against the house's adobe wall. Even though it was only February and the air chilly, the wall radiated heat. Back in San Antonio, Jemmy thought, planting would begin soon. How he wished that he could be there! "I am worried, *amigo*, and my soul is sick with it. You heard Doc Covey? He says we're moving out tomorrow, and I gots to go. But Willie? He ain't able bodied. What with that arm, he cain't drum. And he's too young to shoulder a firearm. So, I'm asking you: Will you keep Willie? Keep him safe and let him heal 'til I come back this ways? I'll collect him on my way home, when this war's ended."

Fungillo nodded thoughtfully. "These injured men that lay on *el piso de me sala*: They are not going with you?"

Jemmy shook his head. "Doc Covey says they'll stay put until they're either healed enough to join us or dead enough to bury."

"But Arsenio, his brother will return for him soon. He will go home and his Mama will care for him."

Jemmy shrugged. "'Spect so."

Fungillo leaned his head against the wall. His eyes studied the cloudless sky, but his mind seemed to be far away, thinking of something else. "My friend, I am thinking that Willie will be better off if he goes with Arsenio. The two are such good *compadres*. He will be happier with them."

Jemmy felt his throat tighten, even as he nodded in agreement. Although Willie would be happier if he stayed with his friend, the idea of leaving the little drummer boy in the care of a man he had shot at worried him. Raul had been generous, telling his brother that Jemmy could be trusted. Could Raul be trusted not to punish Willie for Jemmy's actions?

Chapter Twelve
The Fighting Parson

Cian Lochlann
Denver, Colorado Territory
Tuesday, October 22, 1861

The tack room that Samuel Cook had designated the Company's guard house was exactly nine paces wide by six paces deep. Cian knew this because he'd paced the room over and over since he, E.D Pillier, and Luther Wilson had been thrown into it. The room lacked windows, and although some starlight shone through the loose-slatted walls, it was not nearly enough to illuminate the room. It also wasn't enough air flow to keep three bodies from heating it up. Cian had taken an overly-large stride and slammed face-first into a wall more than once. Each time he did it, his temper rose a notch higher.

"Luther, you idgit!" Cian shouted, holding his throbbing nose, "Why did you have to go and get us thrown in the hoosegow?"

Luther snorted, which wasn't enough of a reply by half as far as Cian was concerned. Cian slugged the wall, and then hopped around, holding his aching hand. "George was boring me to death in our room, but you go and get me confined to an even worse place. I cannot see. I cannot sleep. The straw on the floor is crawling with vermin. Jaysus, but I would thrash you if I could find you."

"That would not be advisable, Private Key." There was ice and steel in Luther's voice as he said the word 'private,' and it gave Cian pause. "Striking an officer is a capital offense. Hit me and the Army will see you hanged or shot."

Cian threw himself down on the ground in a fit of despair. "I want out, I tell you!"

He heard Luther chuckle in the darkness. "Well, Key, that can be arranged."

Cian heard wood slide over wood. A triangle of starlight appeared on the back wall. "What the...? Luther!? How did you know about this?"

"Sam—Captain Cook to you—commanded me to figure out how men who were supposed to be in the guardhouse kept showing up in town. I did as ordered, and I found this. But Sam didn't ever get around to commanding me to fix it. Come on; let's go into town and have us some fun."

Cian got down on hands and knees. He crawled through the hole, then stuck his head back in. "You coming, E.D.?"

"No, sir," the voice in the dark said. "I have been confined to the guardhouse. I plan to stay confined until orders release me."

"Have it your way." Luther Wilson crawled out and the loose board dropped back into place behind him, swinging on its nail like a pendulum.

Cian followed at Luther's heels, hope welling in his heart. He was bored enough to give even Luther, who had treated him badly, a second chance. Maybe Luther would know where there was a poker game going on. Da had taught him to play poker. Or maybe he and Luther would find a saloon with a good piano player and they could sing the night away, like he and his parents used to do in the Boston pubs that catered to the Irish. Anything was better than sitting in Buffalo House and listening to George whine about being a sergeant.

Denver's outlying buildings were dark and quiet, but music and laughter spilled out of McGaa street. Light from many windows painted yellow squares in the dirt road. Pianos punctuated the murmurs of crowded saloons. Cian felt his face go red. Fancy ladies, those women who sold their favors to men, leaned over the balustrade of the closest building. Cian took in their tight, lacy dresses and the careless way their hair was piled on their heads. Some even had rouged cheeks and lips. He stopped walking and kicked at the dirt.

Luther Wilson looked back over his shoulder and grinned. "What is wrong, Key? Afraid these ladies won't treat you right?"

"We are looking for a poker game, right?" Cian's voice came out as a squeak.

"Think again," Luther answered.

"A saloon, so we can join in some singing?"

"Pshaw. Who do you think I am? Your nursemaid? Your daddy?" Luther threw back his head and laughed, then proceeded down McGaa Street. Cian walked back to the edge of town, kicking up clouds of dirt. Sam Cook.

Samuel Logan. George Nelson. Luther Wilson. Da. The more he thought of them, the more he wanted to punch something, anything, but his hand still hurt from punching the wall in the tack room.

Cian slumped onto the wooden walkway in front of a boarding house. "Sam is a schemer, Logan is a bully, George is a fool, and Luther is just plain mean. Jaysus, Mother Mary and all the Saints! 'Tisn't there one good man out there that I could follow?"

"The LORD looked down from heaven upon the children of men, to see if there were any that did understand, and seek God. They are all gone aside, they are all together become filthy: there is none that doeth good, no, not one." Cian recognized the voice that came from behind him. The deep, strong voice resonated with authority. It was the officer who had sent him to the guardhouse. Cian turned around and saw the man, his forearms resting on the boarding house windowsill, his broad shoulders filling the window. The room behind him was lit, so Cian could see sideburns framing a round face that was lost in shadow.

"Psalm 14," the officer continued. "For all have sinned and fall short of the glory of God. Romans 3:23. Soldier, if you are looking for a man to lead you, but they have all let you down, perhaps you should stop looking for a man and start looking to God."

"Ever since me Da died..." Cian began, but his voice trailed off. How could he explain to this stranger how lost he felt?

"God is the protector of the orphan. Trust in Him and be saved. You will come to chapel Sunday morning, where I shall explain further."

"Yes, sir. Thank you, sir," Cian stumbled over his words, awed by how easily this man demanded his obedience.

The man leaned out of the window, studying Cian's

face intently. "Are you one of the soldiers I confined for shooting that herd of cattle earlier this evening?"

"Me, sir? No, sir! I would not be here if I was. I shall be going now, sir." Cian snapped a sharp salute, which the man in the window returned, then he fled down the street. His heart pounded. Back at the guardhouse, he slipped the loose board aside and crawled inside.

"You still here?" Cian asked the darkness.

"I told you I would be," E.D. answered. "Why are you back? Lieutenant Wilson get tired of you?"

Cian snorted derisively. "You could say that. Abandoned me to enjoy the fancy ladies. Then I talked with a man who convinced me I was better off here. I don't know who he is: big, booming voice. Speaks with authority. The one who put us in the guardhouse."

"Ah, you mean the fighting parson."

"Fighting parson?" Cian asked.

"Reverend Major Chivington. He used to be a missionary to the Indians. Governor Gilpin asked him to be the Chaplain of the 1st Colorado Volunteers, but he refused. Said he wanted to fight instead. I heard that he used to preach with a pistol propped on each side of his Bible so no one would argue with him. I also hear that all the enlisted would follow him into the maw of hell if he asked it of them, though I am not sure."

Cian threw his head back. It thumped against the wall. "A parson, you say. And me, being a Catholic. Still, I suppose I could go on Sunday, listen to what he has to say." He sighed. "Everything is going wrong. All I wanted to do tonight was come talk with you. Instead, I get thrown in the hoosegow, get abandoned by Luther, and nearly identified by a Major who could get me court-martialed for escaping this rat-infested hole."

"Sounds like you need a bit of cheering up. You heard

this one yet?

> *We live in hard and stirring times,*
> *Too sad for mirth, too rough for rhymes;*
> *For songs of peace have lost their chimes,*
> *And that's what's the matter!*
> *The men we held as brothers true*
> *Have turned into a rebel crew;*
> *So now we have to put them thro',*
> *And that's what's the matter!*
> *That's what's the matter,*
> *The rebels have to scatter;*
> *We'll make them flee, by land and sea,*
> *And that's what's the matter!"*

E.D.'s clear, rich baritone, filled the air. Cian smiled and joined in, his tenor blending beautifully, and he felt at peace. Tomorrow would be another day, and no matter how it went, he had E.D. to help him through it.

CHAPTER THIRTEEN
ADIOS

Jemmy Martin
Socorro, New Mexico
February 27, 1862

Fungillo put his hand over his eyes and peered into the busy street. "My friend, they are hitching up the last of the teams. You will be leaving soon. I had better bring Raul so he can take the boys home."

Jemmy nodded. "*Mi amigo.* You have been more than kind and patient with us all. I hope we have left all your cooking pots and haven't smashed any of your plates. I will remember you forever." He stuck out his hand.

Fungillo took it and held it. His grip was tight and warm.

Jemmy watched his new friend walk up the road before he made one last circuit through the room. He knelt next to a pallet that contained a soldier who had lost a leg after a minie ball shattered his knee and offered a ladle of water.

The soldier's hands shook, spilling some of it down the front of his shirt. "This is it? You are going?" The look in the soldier's eye, desperate and frightened, made Jemmy's heart ache.

"They'll keep me going so long as I kin hold a rifle and change dressing on a wound. The fightin's behind you now. Soon as they can spare a wagon, you'll be going home."

Home. The very word made Jemmy's spirits sink. It'd been so long since he'd been home that Jemmy couldn't remember the sound of his brother Drew's voice or the smell of his Ma after she'd spent a long day in the kitchen beating biscuits. He almost envied the legless soldier. A leg seemed a small price to pay. He'd be willing to crawl home, if he could.

The soldier shook his head. "Don't seem worth it, coming all this way just to lose a leg. I don't know if I shot me a single Yankee."

"People back home will think you a hero anyhow. I bet the whole town will be baking you pies." Jemmy saw uncertainty and hope play across the wounded soldier's face. He moved on to the next man, who scrambled to his elbows, grabbing the ladle and downing the water in loud gulps.

"Tastes good. When is vittles?" he said, handing the ladle back.

"Soon. The cooks are making up a big mess of beans and cornbread from provisions they found in one of the houses 'round here. Got a couple of sheep up on spits, too.

You'll eat good today."

"Good. Gotta get my strength back up. I wanna get back in the fight and kill me some more Yanks soon as I kin. You, too?"

Jemmy's cheeks burned. "Nope. Not me."

The man frowned. "I guess we needs men to patch us up just as much as we needs men to mow down the enemy," he said, but Jemmy could see the derision in his eyes.

Jemmy stood up. He handed the ladle and bucket to a soldier with a bandaged forearm and a heavy limp. The walking wounded would have to take over the cooking and nursing duties. Those of sound body, such as Jemmy, had to move on.

He went outside and studied the sparse line of wagons on the narrow dirt road. Jemmy wasn't sad to leave Socorro. This disorderly collection of mud houses and chicken pens wasn't a town by his standards. Nothing in New Mexico had been. He missed the bustle and business of San Antonio.

"We ready to go, Jemmy?" Wee Willie leaned up against the door frame, looking for all the world like his legs might collapse under him.

Jemmy placed a hand on Willie's dark head. "You're going to stay here. After all, your arm got busted up only four days ago."

Tears pooled in Willie's eyes. "Cain't I go with you?"

Jemmy ached to grab the boy and squeeze him. "I want you to get stronger, heal up. So, I'm going to leave you with Arsenio. We took care of him. Now he'll take care of you. I'll come back for you on the way back down to Texas."

Willie's lower lip sucked in and he shook his head. "I bin abandoned once. That's why I'm an orphan. They put me in a home, said they was coming back someday, but they never did. I ain't going through that again. I'm coming with you."

Jemmy's heart swelled in his chest, aching with love for the little boy. "I ain't got the heart to argue with you 'bout this, but if you want to go north with me, you got to say *adios* to your little *compadre* before we skedaddle. He will be awful lonesome without you."

Willie nodded solemnly, and the two went back into the house and picked their way among the men. Jemmy held his hand out and wiggled two fingers, making them look like someone walking. He hoped the boy understood. "We is leaving now."

Arsenio's eyes brimmed with tears. "*Adios?*"

"*Si*," Jemmy said, "*adios*."

Arsenio's arms shot out, enveloping Willie in a fierce embrace. Jemmy watched Willie blanch and knew that the hug must have jarred Willie's broken arm, but the drummer boy squeezed his eyes shut and held in any groan that might have embarrassed his friend. When Arsenio released Willie, he said something very solemn, something that Jemmy assumed was thanks, and a hope that they would meet again. Jemmy hoped the same thing, although he was sure that such a meeting would never occur.

Just as they were about to leave, Fungillo stepped into their path. Raul was with him. "You are taking the little one with you after all?"

Jemmy nodded. "He don't want to stay. Scairt of being left behind. Boy don't know what's good for him." Jemmy reached down and ruffled the boy's inky hair.

Fungillo nodded, then turned to Raul and spoke. Raul's face squeezed in thought and he nodded.

"*Ya estamos en paz,* " Raul said, and put a small parcel wrapped in a corn husk into Jemmy's hand..

"*Paz?*" Jemmy repeated.

"The word itself means peace," Fungillo explained, "but it is a saying. *Ya estamos en paz* means now you are, how you say? Even? Square?"

Jemmy shook his head. "Tell him he didn't owe me anything. It was a privilege and a joy to care for his brother." He held out the parcel, but Raul shook his head and walked away.

Fungillo shrugged his shoulders and smiled. "You will not insult his honor by making him take it back. *Vaya con Dios, mi amigo.*"

Jemmy watched the two walk away. He turned to Willie, who was looking up at him with expectant eyes. "Well, little britches, we'd better get a move on. I wonder if we kin catch up with Norvell and Wade?" He shaded his eyes and looked down the road for the two friends he'd made back in San Antonio when he'd first joined the army.

"Let's shake a leg, then," Willie said, and they did. It wasn't until they were miles away from Socorro that Jemmy unwrapped the corn husk and found a silver American half dime.

CHAPTER FOURTEEN
THEY'RE COMING!

Cian Lochlann
Camp Weld
January 6, 1862

Cian jerked awake to find E.D. Pillier snoring on the bunk next to him. At the far end of the barracks, men argued over their poker hands. Cian smiled up at a spider web drifting lazily in the current in the overhead rafters. For the first time since Mam died, his life had a predictable rhythm. Breakfast, drill, lunch, drill, dinner, and bed. It wasn't perfect: The government still hadn't issued a single paycheck. Uniforms and ammunition were in short supply. Sometimes food ran low and the gravy was as thin as broth. But their commanding officer, Major John Slough, had posted a letter in the local paper pleading for blankets, and the citizenry of Denver City had come through. Cian was fed, warm, and had someone to watch over him.

He was just dozing off when George Nelson stomped in and threw himself onto the bunk on the other side of E.D. "I am thinking of deserting. Going east. Enlisting in Kansas, like Sam had intended for us in the first place," he said with a sigh.

"Don't do that! We cannot do without you," Cian said. "You find the wood to keep the barracks toasty. And good things to eat when the commissary runs low on supplies. You keep us in line. Without you, we would all be in the stockade."

"That's just it," George said. "The regular army brass says us volunteers are undisciplined. They don't want us in their ranks. When the war really gets started, we'll be stuck here in Denver, acting like town marshals while the regular army gets all the glory."

"Jaysus, that's ironic, considering the town marshals are who we end up fighting the most," Cian said with a snort.

George threw up his hands. "We need a real enemy to fight. I want to be a hero. Then won't my mother be proud?"

Cian and E.D. exchanged a long, sad look. Every week, E.D. wrote while George dictated a letter home. Every letter detailed how hard he worked to make her proud. The few letters he got in return were long lists of complaints. The weather at the homestead was always too cold or too hot, too rainy or in the middle of a drought. Crops failed. Mice ate what little corn had been harvested. And always, George wasn't providing enough for them. After each letter, George's big shoulders slumped in defeat. He remained listless for days. Cian wished George would cut the apron strings that bound him to his ungrateful mother.

"Wait a wee bit longer, George. Somet'ing is bound to happen."

And just like that, the door to the bunkhouse slammed open and a breathless Luther Wilson rushed in. "Get your gear! We're riding out! Scouts have reported movement near Fort Bliss. The Confederates are invading New Mexico!"

The calm and orderly life Cian had enjoyed dissolved into a chaos of packing and weapons inspections, all accompanied by the excited shouting of orders. Cian mounted Henrietta, the splotched hinny, and Captain Cook's company moved south through the first big snow of the season to join several other companies at Fort Wise, a shabby collection of mud and stone buildings on the north bank of the Arkansas River. Here on the flat plains, the mountains that had loomed so large in Denver looked like blue points on the western horizon. To the east, Cian was sure he could see all the way to Kansas. As the wind howled and sculpted the fallen snow into long, sharp ridges, Cian and the others cut up their wagon boxes to feed the fires that kept them warm. By the end of the month, most of the other companies had been ordered south, to Taos and Santa Fe.

"Our time will come! We will be heroes!" Samuel Cook said.

Luther Wilson snorted. "When? Captain Dodd's Company is more than halfway to Fort Craig and here we sit."

"They pulled their baggage wagons through snow drifts three and more feet deep. You really want to join them?" E.D. said from where he huddled in a dark corner, his knees drawn to his chest and his arms around his shins.

"At least they're not sitting here, burning their own

wagons," Luther answered.

"Ain't my fault! Ain't a tree for miles! We had to burn something," George answered.

Cian looked around at the assembled men and squirmed uncomfortably. He had thought they were finally going someplace, and here they sat, listening to Samuel Cook, who sat near the stove as he told tall tales of his adventures in the Rockies. Sam's brags were always bigger than Cian's recollections.

Cian left the stove's warmth and joined E.D. "You wanting your own company this evening?"

"You are welcome to join me, but I shall not be a brilliant conversationalist tonight."

Cian laughed. "As if any of them are." He thrust his chin forward, indicating the men around the stove. "Penny for your thoughts?"

E.D. sighed and stretched out his legs, staring as his knees as if he were surprised to find them there. "Ever wonder if you made the right choice, joining up?"

"No," Cian said. "I joined up to be fed, and for a place out of the weather. So far, 'tis worked to my advantage."

E.D. nodded. "Fair enough. Don't you miss your kin?"

Cian shook his head. "Don't have any. Me Da disappeared soon after a gang of thugs threatened to beat him up for taking their jobs. We assume they murdered him, but his body was never found. Mam died of the cholera the year I turned fourteen. If I have any other relatives, they're distant, and back in Ireland."

E.D. laid a hand on Cian's arm. "I'm sorry. I never asked. I didn't know."

"But you?" Cian interrupted before E.D. could stammer any other apologies. "Missing kin tonight, are you?" It seemed like Cian waited for ages while E.D. stared at something long ago, far away, and out of sight.

Finally, he spoke. "Lots of kin. I am fourth of ten children. My father and mother came out to the territory to find a better place to raise us. They found it, but my older brother will inherit it, not I. They wanted me to become the family scholar; to teach school. Maybe even college."

Cian let out a laugh. "Why'd you join the Army, then? Last I heard the Army was not turning out college professors."

E.D. shook his head. "Lecturing in a dusty hall is not what I want. I want to buy a farm in Burlington; one just like the one I was raised on. I want to marry a good woman like my mother, raise a brood of my own. I want what my parents had. I planned to use my wages to procure it."

"I never lived on a farm," Cian said.

"I can tell you; it is a little bit of heaven here on earth. Watching your plants come out of soil you tilled, while the sun pops over the horizon. Milking your own cows. Watching the chicks peep after the hens."

"I would like to try that one day," Cian said.

E.D. nudged Cian with his shoulder. "Come visit me in Burlington after the war. Stay as long as you want."

"You would let me milk a cow?"

E.D. laughed. "If you wanted to."

They sat in silence for quite some time, each lost in thoughts of cows and corn coming up, and what the future would hold.

"And how about you, Cian? What were you planning to do after the Army? Go back to Boston?" E.D. asked.

Cian shrugged. "I hadn't really thought that far. I do know I won't be going back east. *No Irish Need Apply* signs hang in shop windows, factory gates, and workshop doors. They don't want my kind there. Got too many of us already. Ever since me Da died, I've felt adrift. I thought in the army I might find someone to follow. Someone strong.

A leader."

"Then you found a leader in Sam?"

Cian shook his head. "Sam Cook is more of a schemer than a leader. I knew that even before I joined up. I thought once about following Samuel Logan, but he was a little too brash. I hear he bullies his men. And Colonel Slough? He may be in charge of us all, but he is a pompous old politician who thinks too highly of himself from what I can see."

"How about Chivington?" E.D. asked.

"The fighting parson? He has backbone. And principles. Remember how he talked me back into that guardhouse the night we shot up that herd?"

E.D. chuckled. "That was a night to remember, all right. I shall never forget how he rallied the troops back at Fort Weld when we were near to mutiny."

Cian leaned the back of his head against the wall and thought about the day when the troops first learned that Gilpin scrip, the paper money that Governor Gilpin had printed to pay them, was worthless. Had Major Chivington not stepped onto a packing crate and delivered a rousing speech about the moral imperative of supporting the Union, the entire Army might have walked out of camp and never returned.

Cian had listened to Chivington with tears coursing down his cheeks. He had been convinced, at least for the moment, that doing the right thing was more important than being paid, and that suffering deprivation in the cause of justice and liberty was noble. He had even gone to Chivington's Sunday sermons, crossing himself at all the wrong times but trying very hard to fit in.

"You are right, E.D. I could follow the Major. But he is still back at Camp Weld, and we are here in the middle of nowhere. You think we shall meet up again?

"I have no doubt of that," E.D. said. "We're not out here

for no good reason, and the state of Colorado hasn't fed us, clothed us, and given us weapon just to let us linger. But if you need something, or someone to inspire you while we wait, I might have just the thing for you." He reached into his saddlebag and rummaged around before dropping a paperback book into Cian's lap. Cian flipped to the title page, which read:

LIFE AND ADVENTURES
OF

KIT CARSON,
THE
NESTOR OF THE ROCKY MOUNTAINS,
FROM FACTS NARRATED BY HIMSELF.
BY DE WITT C. PETERS, M.D.,
LATE ASSISTANT SURGEON U.S.A.
WITH ORIGINAL ILLUSTRATIONS,
DRAWN BY LUMLEY, ENGRAVED BY N.
ORR & CO.

"All are but parts of one stupendous whole, Whose body nature is, and God the soul."

"Kit Carson?" Cian asked.

"Surely, you've heard of him? The greatest mountain man and tracker who ever lived." E.D. took the book from Cian and flipped through the first few pages until he found the words he wanted to point out with his finger. "Says here he is a man of 'sober habits, strict honor, and great regard for truth.' If there's anyone you should choose to follow, by way of example, he's the man."

"I'm not much of a reader," Cian admitted. "Mam taught me letters, and how to read the Bible, but the schools in Boston wouldn't teach the Irish."

"Now, when we're stuck here for who knows how long is as good a time as ever to get in some practice. And this book is as good as any to practice on," E.D. said.

Cian sighed and leaned against the wall next to his friend. He propped the book on his knees and began reading.

CHAPTER FIFTEEN
THOUGHTS OF HOME

Jemmy Martin
Ten miles north of Socorro, New Mexico
February 29, 1862

Left, right, left, right. Jemmy stared at the scuffed and worn toes of his boots as he and Willie plodded north along the Camino Real next to John Norvell and Frederick Wade. He mused on how Pa'd strap him if he saw the condition of those boots. But there was nothing to be done for it. Any grease the Confederate Army had went to feed troops or keep the supply wagon wheels turning. None to spare for shining boots.

Despite its fancy name, the Camino Real, the highway of the old Spanish king was really nothing more than a dusty track that rose and fell over undulating hills. Always, the Rio Grande, the river that was the lifeblood of the land, sparkled on their right. Leave the river, one of the marchers had said, and they would die.

"Where are we? Are we getting close to where we're stopping?" Willie asked.

Frederick stroked his mustache before gesturing at a few adobes clustered in the middle of some fields. "Know what I heard? Someone else told me that this little collection of shacks goes by the grand-sounding moniker of La Polvadera de San Lorenzo."

"Just because you was a school teacher before the war don't mean you have to use such high-fallutin' words," John grumbled. "What's a moniker?"

"A name," Frederick answered. "Know what *polvadera* means? Dusty!"

"It is that," Jemmy said, looking down at his boots.

"We gonna stop at La Dusty de San Lorenzo?" Willie asked.

Jemmy shook his head. "I don't expect we will. We's only been marching, what? Ten miles?"

"I wish we'd camp here for the night. I's tired and my feet hurt. Think we're in for a fit here? Any shooting as we go past?" Willie asked. Jemmy couldn't tell by his tone whether he was anticipating a battle or dreading one.

"Doubt it," John Norvell said. "Doubt any resistance of any sort until at least Albuquerque. They say that's where the Federals are gathering. They say that's where all the Federals supplies are, too! So it's likely there'll be yer fit. I cain't wait! I'll be shooting me some more blue backs!"

Jemmy felt irritation prickle the back of his neck. John Norvell had been full of bravado until he'd encountered the enemy at the Battle of Valverde. Then, he had been shaky and sullen. But as time passed, he'd forgotten just how rattled he'd been, and he'd become full of bravado once again. Jemmy was tired of John's prattle. Tired of Willie's prattle, too. He just wanted to be left alone with his thoughts. He glared at John. "Who's they what says all this?"

John shrugged. "Don't know. Just heard it around."

"I wouldn't trust anything I just heard around," Jemmy said. "Rumors is all it is. Jest as likely invented by the jabberer than true."

John Norvell threw up his hands. "I don't aim to be bothersome, Little Britches. A man's gotta have something to chew on. The march gets long without talking." Jemmy scowled at him even harder, so he quickened his pace and joined the group of soldiers ahead of them. Good riddance to bad rubbish, Jemmy thought.

"You didn't have to be so hard on him, son," Frederick Wade said. He quickened his pace, leaving Willie and Jemmy behind.

"A fit in Albuquerque!" Willie said. "You suppose we'll be in on it?"

"You're in no shape to be in on anything. And I'm not inclined to shoot any Federals, even there," Jemmy said. "I just want to go home."

Willie shrugged, then flinched with the pain he'd inflicted on himself. "I guess if I had a home to go to, I would want to go home, too. But I have none, so I will continue following the army wherever it leads. That way, at least I get fed."

Jemmy's heart ached for Willie, so far from the Louisiana swamps where he'd begun life, so vulnerable after his mother and father's death. He wrapped his arm around the boy's shoulders and gently, so as not to hurt the broken arm, pulled him into his side. "You got a place to go home to, Willie. I swear to you: When this war is over, you are coming home with me."

"What's it like back home?" Willie asked.

Jemmy sighed. "It's a little bit of heaven in the Texas hills. We got us a stream what runs through our land that flows clear and cold all year long. And chickens and a couple pigs and two cows. We used to have a couple mules as well, but you know what happened to Griffith and Golphin."

"Ain't your fault they went over to the enemy," Willie said. "Any mule would of done the same, considering the explosion. Tell me again about the food. Tell me again about how your Ma's going to welcome me."

Jemmy smiled and ruffled Willie's raven-black hair.

"Ma is going to love on you," Jemmy said. "She's always been partial to boys. That's why God gave her two. She's going to fill you up on biscuits and corn bread. Why, I bet she'll wring the neck on one of them chickens and cook her up with gravy just to honor you when you get there."

"An' a pie? She gonna bake me a pie?" Willie looked up at Jemmy, his eyes shining. He had to rub his lips with the back of his hand to keep the saliva from running down his chin.

"'Course she's going to bake you a pie. Peach, I'm guessing. But if we get there before the peaches ripen up, it may be dried apple pie. Or pecan. Or a chess pie. That's what Ma makes when she doesn't have any fruit."

"Maybe she'll make us one of each, she'll be so happy to see us," Willie said.

"Maybe," Jemmy added. And though he smiled for Willie's sake, his stomach clenched as he wondered whether anyone at home would be happy to see him if he didn't bring back Griffith and Golphin.

"Know who I miss? My little *compadre*. You think

we'll see Arsenio ever again? What do you think he's doing right now? Think he's back home? Or is he still with Fungillo? He was nice, too, warn't he?"

Willie's babble ran past Jemmy's ears like water in a stream. When it stopped, Jemmy looked at Willie, who looked back at him, his eyes full of questions. "Ain't that right, Jemmy?"

Jemmy sighed, realizing that Willie had asked him a question. Or maybe a dozen questions. He hadn't been listening. "You tired, Willie? We kin stand to the side and wait for Doc Covey to catch up. Then you kin ride in the hospital wagon."

Willie shook his head. "I ain't tired. I could walk all day, long as I got you to talk with."

Jemmy took a deep breath. It was going to be a long walk indeed.

CHAPTER SIXTEEN
BACK TO CHIVINGTON

Cian Lochlann
Fort Wise
February 22, 1862

Cian sat close to the stove, his lips moving as he formed the words in the book on his knees. Before he went on guard duty, E.D. had said he expected a full report on Kit Carson when he returned. Cian would be ready. Doctor Peters' book was quite the page turner! Cian loved that the doctor described Carson as a little man. It gave him hope that he, too, could make his mark on the world, for although Carson's stature was small, his adventures were enormous.

Outside, the wind wailed and howled, piling up drifts

that looked like little versions of the Rocky Mountains. Cian thought there was no point in sending anyone out to guard in weather like this. Surely no one, not even a wily Comanche, would attack such a puny outpost as Fort Wise in the middle of a snowstorm. But there was nothing that could be done about it. Each of them, including E.D., had watch duty sometime.

Cian looked up when the door blew open, bringing in a maelstrom of snow and his friend. Snow crusted E.D.'s right side, making him look as if he had lain in a snowbank. Cian set aside his book and leapt up, fighting the wind to close the door. The room went so silent that Cian heard the fire crackling in the stove.

E.D. snapped a salute that made the snow slough off the side of his face. His lips were blue, and he shook all over. "C-c-c-captain Cook, sir, I saw a rider coming up from the south."

"Just one?" Samuel Cook rose so quickly that his chair fell back behind him. Most of the other men rose to their feet, too.

"Yes, s-s-s-sir. As far as I can tell, sir. The snow hampers visibility."

Captain Cook nodded, then pointed to several of the men lounging by the fire. "You: Take over Pillier's watch duty. And you six: Mount up and meet that rider. If he's not Union, take him into custody. You, Pillier: come stand here by the stove. You look half-froze."

Cian handed E.D. a mug. "Who do you think it is?"

E.D. shrugged and took a long slug of coffee. "We shall know when he tells us." It did not take long before the men returned, stamping their feet and slapping their own arms to get the snow off. Two of them held up the exhausted rider between them.

"E.D. was right about the visibility," one of the men

said. "By the time we men were saddled up, Lieutenant Graves, here, was almost upon us."

Lieutenant Graves looked up, and his bleary eyes fixed and focused on Samuel Cook. He drew himself up as best he could and gave a rather weak excuse for a salute. "Sir, I'm part of a relay from Fort Union. I have an urgent message for Colonel Slough. If you would present me to him..."

Samuel Cook shook his head. "He's not here. Last I heard, he'd gone back to Camp Weld."

The lieutenant's knees buckled, and his head snapped back. Cian was sure he was on the verge of collapse. Hands quickly pulled off the man's frozen boots and coat, wrapped him in a blanket and handed him a tin mug of whiskey mixed with hot water. Captain Cook motioned to Luther Wilson, who brought up a chair for the lieutenant to collapse onto.

The lieutenant's lips were blue. His teeth chattered. "Colonel Canby thought he was on the march, had predicted he would be here."

"Our Colonel Slough isn't one to suffer the extremities of weather nor the depredations of camp life," Cook said. "Not without good reason."

Lieutenant Graves gripped the cup in hands that shook so violently that the whisky sloshed onto the blanket. "There is good reason. Plenty good. I have important news. It needs to get through. My horse is spent. If you could loan me a fresh mount, I will continue to the next relay station."

Cook shook his head. "The closest relay station is fifteen miles away. How long have you been in the saddle?"

"Six hours."

"Sending you out would mean your death. Let us get you warmed up. We can decide what to do in the morning."

"My message will not wait until morning."

"I cannot see where you have much of a choice," Sam Cook answered.

An idea swirled around in Cian's head. It was as cold and repellant as the snow outside, but just as relentless. Just like Kit Carson, he could be a little man on a big adventure. He could be a hero. "Sam, I can take it to the next relay station."

Samuel Cook frowned. "Have you looked outside, Key? The snow's coming down hard, and it's as dark as a mineshaft."

Cian swallowed hard. "T'is true the drifts are big, and the wind's fierce, but Henrietta is tougher than any horse. If a hinny cannot make it through, nobody can."

Lieutenant Graves reached into his shirt and pulled out a sheaf of papers. "From Colonel Canby, at Fort Craig. The Confederates are lined up on the southern side of the fort. The battle has probably already commenced. Colonel Slough needs to move his forces south, or all will be lost."

Cian nodded and took the papers, stuffing them into his own shirt. As he pulled on gloves and wound a scarf around his neck, E.D. whispered urgently in his ear. "What in heaven's name do you think you are doing?"

Cian shook his head. "Getting closer to Major Chivington." He nodded gravely to Captain Cook and Lieutenant Graves, and rode out into the storm.

CHAPTER SEVENTEEN
ON THE MARCH

Jemmy Martin
South of Albuquerque
March 2, 1862

Jemmy leaned down and poked at Willie's sleeping body. "Morning's here, lazy pants! Time to get up and get a move on! Lookie here what I got you."

Willie stirred. He stretched his fists and yawned. When he opened his eyes, they didn't show the delight that Jemmy had expected—instead, Willie's wide-eyed gaze was filled with terror. "What's that?"

He just couldn't help it, and Jemmy chuckled. "A donkey, silly. I was lucky and traded one of the locals in that little village down there for it. Gave him two sets of socks and my whittling knife. Now you don't got to walk no more."

Willie shook his head. "No, sir. I ain't riding. I will walk alongside you, but there is no way I am getting up on the back of that beast."

Jemmy stared at Willie. "Why not?"

"They is too big for the likes of me. I ain't never been on one, and I do not plan to, now. I will ride in Doc Covey's hospital wagon or walk on my own two feet, but I ain't getting on no horse."

Jemmy frowned. "This ain't no horse, Willie. It's a burro. An' a little one at that."

"I said no, and I meant it," Willie said.

Jemmy shook his head and laughed. "All right, Willie. Then we will continue on our own two feet. You find yer-self some grub at one of the campfires while I give this old girl back. I don't want to try and feed her if she's not going to be of use to us."

The column of men hadn't been on the march more than an hour before the complaining began. "Didn't the General assure us that New Mexicans would welcome us with open arms and open larders?" one of the marchers grumbled. "Said we'd be hailed as saviors, rescuing the people from the Unionists."

"Guess they don't want saving," someone shouted back. Jemmy nodded. Every paltry little farm and village they'd passed had been deserted. He looked up into the surrounding hills and pictured the people sitting up there, surrounded by their chickens and their mattresses, their cooking pots and their carpets, waiting for him and his ilk to pass by. It was kind of funny to think about.

Less funny was how the army had confiscated every bit of flour and cornmeal that remained behind. Although Jemmy had traded for the burro, most of the men in

Sibley's Army had less scruples about how they procured supplies. They'd stolen every chicken, hog, cow or sheep that lingered in pasture or pen and stripped every field and barn of fodder for their mules and horses.

Yet, even after they'd stripped the land bare, they didn't have enough. Jemmy had helped bury four men that morning after he'd returned the burro. Doc Covey wrote in his big register that they had died of pneumonia, measles, and smallpox, but Jemmy was sure that starvation had played a role in their death.

"Poor mule," Willie murmured as they passed another carcass of a pack mule that had been cut from its harness and left to rot on the side of the road. Jemmy diverted his eyes. The way its hip bones and rib cage stuck out sharply beneath the skin made his gut ache. That mule hadn't signed up for this any more than his Golphin and Griffith had. His thoughts wandered back to his mules, and he wondered if they were well fed and watered.

Hope ebbed and flowed in the marchers as news came in from the surrounding countryside. Jemmy's own hopes, which he kept to himself, flowed opposite John Norvell's, who seemed to be looking forward to another encounter with the Union Army. When Norvell's spirits were high, Jemmy's fell and he feared that they would continue north forever. Jemmy was most hopeful when Norvell's spirits were at their lowest.

"What is that, do you suppose?" Willie pointed his good arm west, where a line of dust indicated that something big was heading east. Jemmy squinted through the glare and the dust cloud that his own long, straggling line of wagons and men created, then at the one that Willie pointed toward.

Frederick Wade shielded his eyes with his hand. "Don't know. But if I'm guessing right, they're going to come in contact with our column, two, maybe three miles ahead of us."

"Gots to be one thing or t'other," John Norvell said, practically dancing with excitement. "Might be some of our bummers coming back from a raid. If that's it, everything will be hunkey dorey. If it's t'other, a contingent of Union soldiers from one of their forts, then we will have us a fight on our hands."

"Which fort?" someone behind Jemmy asked.

Another of the men they were walking with, a sergeant, answered. "They got a number of 'em out thataways. Use 'em to fight the Navajo. I was out there myself, posted with the Dragoons at Fort Fauntleroy before this war."

"Only it ain't called Fauntleroy no more," another man said. "Not since Fauntleroy joined the Southern cause. It's Lyons now. But I hear the Army abandoned it."

The sergeant jerked his chin towards the west. "Then tell me where them men is coming from."

The men around Jemmy clutched their firearms a little tighter and marched on in silence. Jemmy felt their emotions roiling from hope to fear and back again. He felt Willie leaning into him as he walked. Jemmy clenched his jaw until his teeth ached. Either supplies or another fight was headed his way. Neither option seemed good to him. He watched the two lines of dust converge, straining his ears for the sound of gunfire. The others must have been doing the same thing, because instead of shots, he heard a hundred men release their breath.

Jemmy watched a messenger riding back through the line, toward him. He sucked in his breath. Good news or bad, he would soon know what was ahead.

CHAPTER EIGHTEEN
RIDING THROUGH A BLIZZARD

Cian Lochlann
February 23, 1862

Cian awoke when his face smashed into the pommel of his saddle. He shook his head, clearing the cobwebs and rubbed his nose with his mittened hand. The mitten came away red with blood. His nose was going to throb when his face thawed out. He shook himself like a dog emerging from water, releasing a puff of snow which hung around him like a cloud.

"Jaysus, Mary and Joseph." The words came out in an icy cloud. Henrietta looked back at him and whinnied softly. She was up to her cannons in snow. He looked around, but saw nothing. All was silent: the howling winds gone, the air clear of snow. How long had he been in the saddle? He was too tired and too cold to think straight.

What was he doing here? For a moment, Cian couldn't remember why he was sitting on a hinny, alone, on a dark night. Then an idea flashed in his head. He thumped his hand against his chest and felt the thick dispatch beneath his shirt. He looked behind him. Henrietta's tracks led into the darkness. Was he going the right way? There were no stars to guide him. No moon. No mountains to tell him west from east. All sign of a trail was obliterated by the snow.

"How long we been standing here? When did it stop snowing?" he asked the spotted hinny. She blinked a brown eye and nickered softly, as if she didn't know how to answer. He responded with another question. "Know which way to go, girl? Because I do not, but standing here, we shall freeze to death." Henrietta's head bobbed and she moved forward. Cian clung to the pommel and peered into the darkness, looking for anything that might guide him to the relay station. Once there, he could hand off the packet to a fresh rider on a fresh horse, then he and Henrietta could thaw out and rest.

He'd heard it said that falling asleep in the cold was an easy way to die, the mind moving farther from reality, as the body got colder. Supposedly, the body stopped feeling the gnawing bite of the cold and began to feel comfortably warm, lulling the mind further into drowsiness. Finally, body and mind drifted into unconsciousness and then death, painlessly and without struggle.

Jemmy shook his head. He wasn't ready for a painless death. Not yet. His thighs and shoulders ached with the cold. Even his teeth hurt. He told himself the pain was good. It meant he was still alive, still had a chance of not succumbing to the cold. He ran his tongue over his teeth while he shook one hand, then transferred the reins into it while he shook the other. His fingers tingled and burned with movement. Cian did it again to convince his hands to keep working. He pulled the scarf higher over his cheeks and tried to flex his toes. Fight the cold. Fight sleep. It was the only way he was going to survive.

Off in the distance to their left, wolves, or maybe coyotes, keened. Henrietta's ears swiveled to listen, then flattened back. She broke into a trot. Cian leaned forward in the saddle and tried to keep alert. If he fell asleep now, he might fall off Henrietta's back. Then he'd be easy prey for whatever it was that was howling.

They converged with a set of wagon tracks and, for lack of a better plan, followed them. Cian hoped, no—believed—they were leading to the relay station. "T'inkin' is believin'," Cian heard his Mam say, and the rocking of the saddle became the rocking of a ship at sea.

He woke again with a start and found that Henrietta was still following the tracks. The clouds had thinned while Cian slept. In their place, a dozen points of light flickered in a sky that was lightening to pearl gray. The last slim crescent of a waning moon hung on the eastern horizon.

And right in front of him, a yellow light glimmered.

Cian's cheeks puffed out in a sigh of relief. Henrietta had seen him through. He leaned down and patted the hinny's neck. "You may be part donkey and part horse, but you must be part homing pigeon, too. How did you manage to find the relay station, old girl?" Henrietta knickered and picked up the pace.

The relay station would have been easy to miss. Just a small barracks and a stable, it was one of a string of stations that dotted the trail between Denver and Santa Fe. A thin wisp of smoke curled from the chimney. Cian smiled and licked his chapped lips at the thought of coffee warming them.

A man came out the door of the barracks and stood, watching Cian ride in. "What are you doing up so early?" he asked as Henrietta trotted up to him.

"Message from Colonel Canby. For Colonel Slough," Cian said.

The man gave a jolt, then opened the door and shouted in that someone needed to get ready to ride north. He turned back and patted Henrietta's neck. "You get down now. Go in and warm up. John can rustle you some grub. I'll take care of this beast for you."

Cian slid off Henrietta's back. He wobbled, hanging on to the pommel as feeling came back into his legs, then hobbled through the door and into the warm room that served as kitchen and gathering place. "John?"

The man at the cookstove looked up and frowned. "Who are you? You're not a regular courier."

"Private Cian Lochlann, First Volunteers, Company F. The courier rode into Fort Wise half frozen last night. I rode the next leg for him."

"Must have gotten lost in the snow. You look half frozen, yourself. Here." He handed Cian a cup of steaming coffee and pulled a chair up to the stove for him. In a moment, a courier came out of the other room, shrugged himself into his coat, took Cian's parcel, and left.

Cian's whole body throbbed. His toes, fingers, and the tip of his nose burned. He couldn't stop shaking. John leaned down and studied the tips of Cian's ears. "You might lose a bit of flesh on the edges. How're your feet?"

"I still got 'em," Cian said. He smiled and took another sip of coffee.

John lifted an eyebrow, then knelt in front of Cian and untied the laces on his brogues. He pulled off Cian's socks, then studied Cian's feet, pinching each toe and watching the color change from blue to pink. "You're lucky. You'll keep all your toes. The skin might peel, and they'll burn for a while, but they aren't frost bit, just chilblained. You're lucky the cold didn't lull you to sleep."

"It did," Cian admitted. "But me hinny kept on going."

"Then you're lucky you've got a mount smarter than her rider. Shuck out of those clothes and I'll get you some breakfast before you get some shut-eye. When you're feeling refreshed, I'm sure Ambrose in the stables can pick out a mount for you to ride back."

"If it's all the same to you, I'd like to take my hinny back," Cian said as his stiff fingers fumbled with the buttons on his jacket.

John frowned while he thought. "Couriers aren't particular about their mounts. They'll ride whatever's freshest. I forget most men are more attached to their regular mounts. We'll take care of yours, but I doubt she'll be ready before tomorrow. If your commanding officer didn't tell you to return quickly, I guess it doesn't matter how long you stay."

Cian smiled. Captain Cook hadn't told him to come back quickly. If his memory served him, Cook hadn't mentioned when, or if, he should come back at all. As Cian considered his options, John set a tin plate full of eggs, fried potatoes, and bacon on his lap. Cian fumbled with the fork. His fingers refused to bend, and it clattered to the ground.

John sighed. "You won't be the first rider I had to feed. Open up."

Cian opened his mouth and John spooned the food in. He felt as fragile and helpless as a baby bird, but the food warmed him from the inside out. Soon, his legs and arms buzzed as the blood returned to them. The warmer he got, the more his head spun. He blinked once, twice, and a third time before drifting off to sleep.

Cian awoke in a bed piled high with blankets. Through the open door, he heard John talking with a couple of other men and the clatter of cooking. He sat up and found his clothes laid out on the foot of his bed, so he slipped into them and padded on stocking feet into the next room.

John looked up from the stove. "You up? Feeling better, Keen?"

"Much, thanks to you," Cian said, ignoring the mispronunciation of his name. John could call him anything he wanted! He'd earned the right by taking such good care of him.

'That's my job. Boys, this here's Keen Lochland. He's with Company F of the First, but they used him as a courier during the storm. Did the last leg when Graves got himself lost in the snow. He'll be going back now."

"My hinny's recovered?" Cian asked.

John snorted. "You've been asleep for more'n twenty-four hours. She's ready to go."

Cian ate a hearty breakfast, said his goodbyes, and mounted Henrietta. But he didn't ride back to Fort Wise. Instead, he traveled west, determined to catch up with Chivington and his men.

CHAPTER NINETEEN
ONWARD TO ALBUQUERQUE

Jemmy Martin
South of Albuquerque
March 2, 1862

"Hoy! You there! What's the word?" Frederick Wade called when the rider came by.

The rider reined in his horse. "Good news, lads! Four men sympathetic to our cause went to the union supply depot in Cubero, and the garrison there surrendered without a fight."

"Where's Cubero?" one of the marchers asked.

The messenger jerked his thumb west. "'bout sixty miles west of here."

"So that dust there?" a voice called from the crowd.

"Was thrown up by the twenty-five wagons of food and supplies we liberated from the supply depot. It's enough to tide us over for forty days!"

John Norvell crowed with joy. "Let's just sit ourselves down right here and have a feast!"

The rider shook his head. "Tomorrow you should be entering Albuquerque. I've heard tell they have a huge supply depot! Enough forage to last Sibley's army six months.

"Well, then! Onward to Albuquerque," the sergeant ordered.

Jemmy found himself having to listen to Norvell, who could not stop talking about their improved prospects. Once they had all that food and fodder, Santa Fe would fall into their laps like a plum ripe for picking! Next, Fort Union, the largest fort in all of New Mexico territory and the last obstacle between them and the Colorado gold-fields! Finally, on to San Francisco and more gold! The Confederacy would be awash in money and prestige! Bringing in such riches and such territory would make them saviors to the cause!

The more John babbled, the lower Jemmy felt. Would he ever have the chance to take Willie home?

That night Jemmy lay awake and listened to men sing with more gusto than they'd exhibited since leaving Texas. Late in the night, he finally fell asleep, but dreamed fitfully of home, of his Ma and Pa and of the two mules he had lost at Valverde. He woke early, stirred up the fire and started coffee, all the while praying for some kind of miracle that would allow him and Willie to turn around and head south. Home, to San Antonio and the little farm where his Ma, Pa, and brother were working without him and without the mules they needed so badly.

"Everyone seems to think today is going to be the

best day of the campaign." The words nearly made Jemmy jump out of his boots. He turned and found Willie standing right behind him. Jemmy grinned and poked the fire with a stick. The orphan drummer boy was aptly named. The way Willie moved silently about camp, the paleness of his face and the mournful depths of his black eyes gave many a man the willies.

"I dunno. If'n there is as much in that supply depot as we hear tell, I expects they'll fight awful hard to keep it."

Willie peered northward, as if he could see Albuquerque if he squinted hard enough. "You think there's going to be another fight?"

Jemmy shrugged. "I ain't the general. How would I know?"

By mid-morning, they had covered half the distance to Albuquerque, and although the town itself remained hidden behind the low, rolling hills, a tall pillar of smoke marked its location. Long before their part of the train arrived, news filtered back that the soldiers guarding the supply depot had set it afire before abandoning the town. The smoke they saw was six months of fodder going up in flames.

Jemmy smiled to himself. Though he had never been an enthusiastic church goer, his Ma had insisted he be a frequent one. He stared at the pillar of smoke and thought about the pillar of clouds that had led the Israelites through the wilderness. He'd been praying for a miracle. Was this the sign that his days of wandering were over and that he could go home?

They pulled into Albuquerque—a dusty little square of adobe buildings not unlike Socorro—just in time to watch the Confederate flag run up the pole. William Davidson, the quartermaster, sat astride his horse, shouting orders and directing traffic while a band played "Dixie" and "The Girl I Left Behind Me." Searching for Doc Covey, Jemmy elbowed his way through the milling troops, with Willie hanging on tight to the back of his shirt. The Doctor and his aides stood near his hospital wagon.

"See that?" the doctor said, jerking his chin toward a pool of grease just in front of the smoldering ruins of the commissary building.

"Yes?" Jemmy answered.

"That is all that's left of the supplies we had been looking forward to. Everything else has been either burned or stolen by the locals before we arrived."

"That mean we can go home?" Jemmy asked, his mood lightening.

Doc Covey shook his head. "We still have the supplies from Cubero. They should keep us going until we take Fort Union."

Finally, the last of the troops straggled into the plaza. Bill Davidson put up a hand to silence them.

"Where are you gonna put us, Old Bill?" the driver on Doc Covey's wagon called.

Davidson took off his hat and wiped sweat from his brow, then pointed a gloved hand east. "Boys, there's not enough fodder in town to feed all our horses. I am splitting the Army. Some will stay here in Albuquerque. Others will go into those mountains, where I hear there is more grass. See that low spot there? That is Carnue Pass. A wagon road goes up through there, then turns north again. Those who are going into the mountains should take that road, then find a suitable place to camp and await further orders. We will reconnoiter in Santa Fe, once we take it."

Davidson started naming off units, pointing this way and that. As they were called, men separated from the crowd to reorganize themselves. Jemmy watched John Norvell and Frederick Wade shuffle into the group heading north to Santa Fe. He twitched with hope that he and Willie could continue with them.

"And you, Doc Covey," Davidson said, looking toward the men standing with Jemmy, then pointing across the plaza, "General Sibley has specifically ordered you to accompany him. He'll billet in the home of Rafael and Manuel Armijo, over there."

"Who will be doctoring the troops going into the mountains, then?" Doctor Covey asked.

Davidson shrugged. "The thinner we spread ourselves, the harder it is to position you docs. The men in the mountains will be on their own until they reach Santa Fe."

Doctor Covey turned to his aides. "I'll keep the wounded and half you men with me. We'll probably find a house here in town to turn into a hospital. The other half of you will go with the boys in the mountains. You'll have the wagon, too, in case any get sick or injured and can't walk. You, you, and you go with the medical wagon. Thomas, I'm putting you in charge. Do what you can to help the boys until we meet up in Santa Fe again." Doc Covey's fingers pointed towards three of his aides, including the tall, gangly one named Thomas. Jemmy blinked in surprise when the doctor pointed to him.

"I'm no aide. I'm a packer," Jemmy protested.

Doc Covey nodded. "I know that, son. But we're spread thin, and I need all the help I can get. I'll meet you all in Santa Fe."

Willie turned to Jemmy as the Doctor walked away and the aides reorganized themselves into two groups. "Doc didn't say where I should go."

"Yer going with me, of course, so's I kin protect you." Jemmy squinted at the low saddle in the mountains. It didn't look too daunting. He was wrong.

CHAPTER TWENTY
FOLLOW THE LEADER

Cian Lochlann
Camp "Shiverington"
February 28, 1862

Cian rode due west, hoping to intercept the army on its march south. On the morning that he saw the smoky haze at the base of Pike's Peak, he knew he must have found it. As he rode closer, he saw horses huddled together amid the tents, their backs to the wind, their heads and tails tucked. The snow, so white elsewhere, had been churned into the mud around the campfires where men huddled, their shoulders hunched against the snow that was still coming down. A man in full uniform stood at the edge of the encampment, a gun held across his chest. Cian rode toward him, his hands out where the sentry could see. He hadn't traveled this far to be shot by his own side.

"Halt! Who goes there?" the sentry called when Cian came within hailing distance.

Cian reined in Henrietta. "Private Cian Lochlann, of Company F, First Volunteers, out of Fort Wise."

The sentry's arms sagged in surprise. "Fort Wise? You rode all that way in this weather?"

Cian nodded sheepishly. "Took me four days, but I did it. Stopped at farmhouses and relay stations to rest, warm meself and get oats for Henrietta, here." Cian leaned down and patted the hinny's neck. Her ears went back as if she were listening to him. "I have a message for Colonel Slough. He here?"

The sentry nodded and pointed over his shoulder. "See the big tent? With the flags flying? That's headquarters."

Cian nodded and nudged Henrietta on. At headquarters, he swung out of the saddle and announced that he had a message from Colonel Canby for Colonel Slough. He didn't bother to add that he'd passed that message on days ago.

"Colonel Slough and his officers are breakfasting and not to be disturbed. They will see you when they finish," one of the two sentries at the entrance to the tent said.

"Emit," the other sentry said in a snarl. "You don't think he rode all that way to sit while the Colonel finished his eggs, do you?"

The sentry's composure crumbled a bit. "But it's orders, Benjamin."

Benjamin sighed. "If a message is important enough to ride that far in this weather to deliver, it's important enough to disrupt breakfast." He pushed his way past Emit, dragging Cian with him.

Cian grinned, pleased that he'd found a way to get

close to the Colonel, because that meant getting close to Major Chivington. Maybe, if he could get the man's attention, Chivington would take Cian under his wing, let him be some kind of aide de camp or messenger. Then Cian would have found the man that could lead him into the future! The very thought of it made Cian's pulse rise.

Inside the tent, a half dozen men, including Colonel Slough and Major Chivington, sat at a rickety camp table. They all looked up, scowling, their knives and forks hovering over plates filled with bacon, eggs, and beans. Cian sniffed the air. His mouth watered and he had to swallow to keep from drowning.

Colonel Slough's voice boomed. "Did you not know we were eating?"

The sentry who had led Cian in snapped off a salute. "Begging your pardon, sir. This private rode all the way from Colonel Canby with a dispatch for you, sir. I thought it must be important."

Colonel Slough snorted. "If he told you he came from Canby, he's lying. That's hundreds of miles away. "But hand it over."

Cian swallowed hard. Suddenly his mouth felt dry. He'd managed to get himself in front of Major Chivington, but he hadn't thought of what to say once he got here. "I, uh, don't have it, Sir. I handed it on at a relay station."

Colonel Slough raised one eyebrow.

The irritation in his eyes made Cian's heart jump to his throat. "I followed after, Sir, to make sure that it was delivered. It was important."

"And what was this important message?"

"It was from Colonel Canby, Sir. At Fort Craig. He said the Confederate forces were on the southern side of the fort and lined up for battle, and that you needed to move your troops south immediately or all would be lost."

Colonel Slough snorted. "Yes, your message was delivered, and it's old news now. The battle's over."

"Did we win?"

The Colonel scowled at him. Cian studied the tops of his boots and wished that he had thought this through a little better.

"No, son. We didn't win." Cian recognized Major Chivington's deep but gentle voice. "We held the fort, but lost many good men. Captain McRae died defending his guns, which are now in the possession of the enemy. And all but two of Captain Dodd's men were killed."

"Our Captain Dodd? Company A?" Cian felt his eyes bugging out from his head. He knew those men. Company A had bunked with Captain Cook's men at Fort Wise. How could they be dead?

"Yes, son. Our Captain Dodd." Major Chivington dabbed at the egg yolk stuck in his mustache, then scooted back his chair. "Sentry, find this lad some breakfast. After that, find him a place to rest. He had a long and difficult ride, wherever he came from. He will need his strength if he is to join us on the ride back to Colonel Canby."

Cian snapped a sharp salute before following the sentry out of the tent. He wanted to whoop and holler. He had talked with Chivington! Now, he was going to ride south with the Major. This could be the break he was waiting for.

"I don't know where we're going to put you," the sentry said as he led Cian away. "The night after we left Denver, we discovered there were only enough tents for about a third of us. We've been hunkered down here for three days now, waiting for this vicious storm to pass. We've taken to calling the place "Camp Shiverington.""

"I've suffered worse," Cian said. "I used to be a miner."

"Oh! You're one of the Pike Peakers, eh? You're a tough bunch," the man said. The glow of speaking with the man they called The Fighting Parson and the admiration in the sentry's words warmed Cian from the inside out. He accepted a plate of beans at one of the campfires, but no one could find in a place in a tent. Finally, when the best anyone could offer him was a single blanket, he piled snow against the windward side of a wagon, convinced Henrietta to lay down on the leeward side, then crawled under the wagon. He was almost asleep when a pair of well-polished boots came to a stop near his wagon.

A deep voice asked, "Son, are you all right?"

Cian sat up so quickly that he clonked his head into the wagon bed. A thousand stars streaked across his vision like sparks from a campfire. He slouched back down, cupping the sore spot in his hand. "Yes, sir. I am fine, sir."

Major Chivington knelt down, one hand upraised against the wagon. Even in the shadows, Cian could see how piercingly blue his eyes were. "Ah! The courier that rode all the way from Colonel Canby just to make sure his message had been delivered! Rest up, son. We have a long ride ahead of us once this weather clears."

"Thank you for checking on me, sir," Cian said.

The Major nodded. "I'm checking on all the men. I sent six back to hospital in Colorado City for frostbite. I do not want you to be another. We need every man we can get, especially the stubborn and stout-hearted ones like you. The cold has killed some horses and mules, too. I am particularly fond of mules. Do not let anything happen to yours."

"Yes, sir! I won't, sir!" Just knowing the Major cared was enough to make Cian's chest swell uncomfortably. He was a little afraid that he might cry in gratitude. The Major smiled and nodded before he stood back up and walked away. Cian watched his black boots stop at the next campfire. He listened to the deep rumble of Chivington's voice as he inquired of the men surrounding it, and the twang and rumble of answering voices. The boots moved on again before disappearing into the gathering dark. Cian would follow those boots anywhere.

CHAPTER TWENTY-ONE
ANYWHERE DOWN FROM HERE

**Jemmy Martin
Tijeras, New Mexico
Mountains east of Albuquerque
March 12, 1862**

Jemmy lay on his side in his improvised shelter, with Willie curled up between his chest and his drawn-up knees. The shelter, such as it was, consisted of the hospital wagon for a roof, one ratty blanket for a ground cloth, and piles of packed snow for walls. Their combined body heat kept the little space warmer than outside, and so, unless there was something to do, they stayed put in their little twilight nest.

When the quartermaster, William Davidson, had sent

half the Army up through Carnue Pass, he'd said there was more forage for the horses in the Sandia Mountains. Perhaps he was right, but how were they to find it under the two feet of snow that covered the ground? Jemmy had never seen so much snow. This much snow hadn't fallen in San Antonio in his whole life. But, snow or no snow, the men waited, hunkered down with little to do but attempt to keep warm and fed and wait for orders.

Thomas and the other medical aides had buried fifty men during the week they had been in the little village of Tijeras. In spite everything they'd tried to do for them, the men died from smallpox, measles, and pneumonia. Others had succumbed to the cold.

Willie jerked his head back, slamming it into Jemmy's face. "D'ya'll hear that?"

"Hear what?" Jemmy gingerly touched the lip that was surely going to swell.

"Talking. Something is going on out there." Willie scrambled about, pulling on his boots and ramming his hat onto his head. He punched a hole in the snow wall crawled out. Icy bits rained on Jemmy as he followed. Within a circled of gathered men, William Davidson sat astride his horse, a nasty scowl on his face.

"Hey there, Old Bill! Find us nicer quarters?" one of the men in the crowd called, raising laughter from his buddies, who stood around slapping their sides to keep warm.

"We picked this village clean," Davidson replied. "Orders are to divide you men and send you on to better forage." He pulled a sheet of paper from the breast pocket of his jacket and studied it a moment. "Company A of the Fourth: you are going back to Albuquerque."

A small cheer rose up, and men left to begin gathering their belongings.

Davidson studied his paper a moment more before he continued. "Company A of the Seventh: you are headed down to Cubero."

"Down. The word I wanted to hear," A man called. "Anywhere down from here is bound to be warmer."

"It is warmer in hell, and that is down from here, too," another man shouted. The men laughed until Davidson scowled them into silence.

"Pyron's men, Shropshire's men, Phillips' Brigands: you are continuing north to Santa Fe." Davidson scowled some more, and the men who belonged in these units left to pack. Jemmy looked around at the few hundred men remaining.

"What about us?" one of them called. "You are not leaving us here to freeze, are you?"

"'Course not." Old Bill scowled down at his paper for a minute. "You remaining companies of the Fourth and Seventh Regiments are to attach yourselves to Lieutenant Colonel William Scurry. You are the rear guard. You will progress six and a half miles north, to the town of San Antonito, and await further orders."

Willie turned to Jemmy. "What does that mean?"

"It means," Jemmy answered, "that we take our snow fort apart and walk for a day, then crawl back in it and wait some more."

"That does not sound very exciting," Willie said with a sigh.

Jemmy nodded in agreement, but in his heart, he knew that it meant they were that much closer to the enemy, and to another battle.

CHAPTER TWENTY-TWO
ON EAGLE'S WINGS

Cian Lochlann
March 6, 1862

Cian was saddling Henrietta the next morning when a carriage passed by, going north. "And who would that be, all hoity-toity in a carriage?" Cian asked no one in particular.

One of the men loading the wagon under which Cian had slept let out a snort and threw a rolled tent in with a little extra force. "That would be our noble leader, Colonel Slough."

"In a carriage? Going north?" Cian asked.

The man snorted again. "That's right. Just like a lady. A real man would be on horseback, no? Scuttlebutt is, he and Chivington got into an argument on how to proceed. Slough's going back to Colorado City, to wait out the storm in a warm, dry inn. He doesn't think this is the weather for warring in."

The thought made Cian's blood boil. He cinched up a little tighter than he should have. Henrietta swiveled her head, ears back, teeth barred. "Sorry, girl," he muttered, then spoke louder, to the packer. "Aren't leaders expected to suffer along with their troops?"

"That's what Chivington says," the packer answered.

As they rode out of Camp Shiverington, the men joked among themselves about the newspaper editorial that said Slough was leading Governor Gilpin's Pet Lambs to slaughter. It didn't seem funny to Cian. How could Slough lead them anywhere if he was going back in his carriage to a warm bed and a good meal while the rest of the Army slogged south? And, after all this marching, would Slough really be leading them into an impossible situation, where they would be slaughtered? He wished E.D., who listened to him calmly and reasonably and always had a well-thought-out response could talk with him about it. Even Luther and Sam, who could connive and talk their way into or out of anything, or George, who was brave enough or dumb enough—he wasn't sure which—to push forward unquestioningly, would be welcome now. Within this sea of marching men, Cian felt alone.

By noon they had traveled less than ten miles. Cian rode up to find the infantry collapsed by the banks of Greenhorn Creek. "That's it. We're done for the day," one of the sergeants groaned. Cian listened to the men's mutinous grumbling and kept his mouth shut. It was true that the weather seemed against them and that they didn't have the supplies that would have kept them comfortable, warm and fed. But this was war, not a holiday stroll. The conditions were hardly worse than the cold and hunger of the mining camp. These men had grown soft and spoiled on government food and barracks life and, as far as Cian was concerned, it was time for them to earn their keep. The men had rested thirty minutes when a rider passed by, telling the men that Major Chivington demanded that they continue south.

Sundown found them another ten miles farther, on the banks of Dry Creek. The exhausted men threw down their rucksacks, too tired to set up camp or make dinner. Cian scanned the eastern horizon. How close were they to Fort Wise? Would Cook's men be joining forces with them soon?

Something—a spot of darkness amid the white expanse of snow—appeared. Cian blinked twice to make sure he wasn't seeing things. The spot grew larger. Cian sprinted towards the tent that was flying a flag.

"Major Chivington, sir! A messenger!" he shouted as he elbowed his way through the general staff who were setting up tents and starting fires.

Major Chivington's head popped out from beside a half-erected tent. Cian saw the recognition in the Major's blue eyes. "A messenger? From where? And how do you know, son?"

"I saw him, Sir! From the east. I'm guessing Fort Wise." Cian gesticulated back toward where the spot was beginning to resolve into a rider. In just a few minutes, he was close enough that Cian recognized him. "It's one of Lt. Col. Tappan's men, sir! They're at Fort Wise."

The troops who had been too tired to erect their own tents found their legs and gathered around the rider, shouting questions and eager for news. Major Chivington plowed through the men like a schooner through waves, with Cian hot on his heels. The Major grabbed the rider's horse by the bridle and led him through the crowd, bellowing that the men should muster, and that he would give a report as soon as he had heard the courier's message.

The men waited almost cheerily, slapping each other on the back and shuffling their feet excitedly. Cian stood among them, listening to their prattle. Something—finally—was going to happen! After a quarter of an hour, John Chivington appeared again and climbed on a packing crate. He towered over the crowd.

"Men," he said in his loud, booming voice, "Colonel Tappan informs us that the Confederacy has already taken both Albuquerque and Santa Fe. I quote: 'For God's sake, you must hurry on. I fear that we may already be too late. The only hope for Canby and for New Mexico, and ultimately, for the United States, is your timely arrival at Fort Union.'"

John Chivington looked up from the paper he had been reading. His eyes scanned the crowd of men that had gone silent, frozen with shock. His piercing gaze bore into each of them before he continued in a voice that was soft, yet loud enough for everyone to hear. "The disaster that will follow a Confederate victory at Fort Union will be our personal disaster. If the Rebels get Union, there shall be no stopping them in Colorado. And so, I ask you: Are you willing to endure forced marches in order to save the honor and property of the republic?"

The men shouted in a chorus of enthusiasm that made Cian's heart swell with pride.

"Then may God have mercy on us," Chivington said with a nod of approval. "Abandon everything except your weapons, one spare shirt, an extra canteen, two day's hardtack, coffee, and two blankets. Our teamsters will pick up our cast-off baggage and catch up to us when they can. We will make sixty-five miles every twenty-four hours until we reach Fort Union. It is the only way!"

The men gave a great cheer and began packing what they were to carry, piling up the rest. Within an hour, the men who had been too tired to move were on the march. Cian smiled wryly at the men who, reenergized by Chivington's speech, set out singing and boisterous. He wasn't at all surprised when their spirits faded after a few short miles. The march proceeded, silent except for the tramp of feet and the jingle of harness. At 10 o'clock, they stumbled into Camp Sanborn. Even Cian, who prided himself on his scrappy resolve, was exhausted. They had traveled forty-two miles that day. The next leg of the journey, the climb up to Raton Pass, was so steep and arduous that even Chivington thought it better that it be done in daylight. He ordered five hours for sleep.

Cian threw his blankets on the ground and wrapped himself in them. His head buzzed with exhaustion and his body ached. He knew he should choke down some hardtack, but he was too tired to even do that. Three o'clock in the morning, when they were to get up, grab a quick cup of coffee and begin the climb to the pass, seemed too near. Just when he felt himself slip into unconsciousness, a voice, far and distant, brought him back to wakefulness.

"Key? You here, son? Ho! You there! You seen a scrawny Irish kid on a piebald mule?"

Cian sat up groggily, wondering if he was awake or dreaming. "Sam? 's'at you?"

Sam Cook, Luther Wilson, George Nelson, and E. D. Pillier hopped over the dozens of man-filled bedrolls, whooping with delight.

"Huzzah! We found you!" Sam said.

"Got in about 10:30, only no one around here had a clue who you were," Luther added. "Made us wonder if you made it through alive!"

"Now E.D. won't have to write to my Mother about your death," said George. The three continued to talk all at once, each trying to catch Cian up on what had happened since he'd left them and how worried they'd been about him. All the while, E.D. stood by with a foolish grin on his face. Cian grinned back. It was good to be with friends again, and it was especially good to see Sam and Luther not putting on airs over being officers.

"How about you boys grab your bedrolls and join me in some shut-eye? We will have plenty of time to talk on tomorrow's march," Cian said.

"Right! Bedrolls!" The three hopped back over the sleeping troops, leaving E.D., whose bedroll was slung around his shoulders, smiling down at Cian.

"I guess it is evident that we are happy to see you safe and sound," E.D. said as he rolled out his blanket. "We have become like family. I missed you. I brought *Kit Carson, The Nestor of the Rocky Mountains* for you."

Cian smiled even wider. "And I missed you, too, brother." Tomorrow he might read, but for now he was too tired. He closed his eyes and fell asleep to the blissful sounds of E.D.'s snoring.

The troops rustled awake at three in the morning. Cian made a pot of coffee for his friends, happy to not be alone in the crowd anymore. As he handed a cup to Sam, his captain rubbed the bristle on his chin.

"I been thinking, Key. We were awfully sad when we thought you'd died in the blizzard. But now that you're alive, I'm wondering if I shouldn't charge you with desertion? Keep back a little of your pay, maybe."

Cian stood up so quickly the coffee sloshed out of the pot. "Desertion? I didn't desert, Sam. I followed orders and got the message on to the Colonel. Then I joined back up with you the best way I knew how."

"You didn't come back to Fort Wise," Sam said.

"Didn't think you'd be there when I got back," Cian argued.

"Did you even try?"

Cian felt his temper rise. He wanted to argue—wanted to throw a punch, even—but what would be the point? And Sam was his superior. If he argued, he might not only lose is pay, but spend a day walking in chains. Cian had seen a few fellows who'd had to do that. It didn't look comfortable. Cian took a deep breath and let it out slowly to steady himself.

"Captain Cook, sir, if I'd wanted to absquatulate, I would've been halfway to California by now, instead of here with the army. But if you think you need to hold back some of my pay because I didn't return as fast as expected, I accept that." He moved away, filling the cups of the other men who huddled around his campfire.

"Smart move. Especially since we haven't been paid since we left Denver anyway," E.D. said in a low voice when Cian filled his cup.

By four o'clock in the morning, they were on the move. Cian watched the sky lighten as he climbed. The trail was so steep that most men led their mounts instead of riding them. Sometimes a dozen men had to line up behind the few Fort Wise wagons and push while the mules in front strained to pull. Despite the struggle, Cian felt lighter at heart. He had his friends, and he hadn't gotten into a fight with Sam. Maybe he was finally becoming a man that he could be proud of.

That night the company slept near a beaver dam halfway up the pass. The clouds cleared, revealing a million stars that glittered so beautifully in the icy sky that Cian almost forgot how cold he was. The next morning, dawn came late, hidden by the eastern peaks. When sunlight finally filled the pass, the reflection off the snow was so brilliant that the men had to squint. Many became snow-blind.

Cian reached the top of the pass at midday. Below him, the plains spread out, a vast expanse of white snow and yellowed grass.

"There it is. New Mexico," Sam Cook said. "Doesn't look any different than eastern Colorado, do it?"

"Certainly not worth fighting for," Luther Wilson said. "I say we let the Rebs have it."

"Nope. We need to keep New Mexico as a buffer zone. It keeps the Rebs off our back stoop," E.D. said.

"Lookie there!" George pointed almost straight up, where two bald eagles circled on an updraft of air. "A silver dollar to the first man who brings one down!"

Instantly a hundred muzzles pointed skyward.

"Halt!" a voice called. Cian turned to see Captain Downing, red-faced with the exertion of the climb, holding up his hand. "These are the birds of liberty! They betoken victory for us. Let us give three cheers for the eagles, then proceed on."

"Well, hell's bells. I only meant to raise the men's morale," George said.

"Don't matter. It's all downhill from here. That should raise morale," E.D. said. The men gave three cheers, then moved down the mountainside.

Luther snorted. "Morale would 'a come down significantly when those bullets did. Them eagles were nearly directly above us."

"Had not thought of that," George conceded.

"Had not thought how steep this hill was, neither," Cian said. If pushing the wagons up the hill had been hard work, hanging on to the backs of them so that they didn't run over their own draft mules was even harder. The men in the front of the column had to wade through snow that was sometimes thigh deep and made slushy by the sun on the southern exposure. Back where Cian was, slippery slush sent the wagons skittering. By the time they were on flat land again, they were exhausted, and the sun had sank beneath the rim of mountains to their west.

The soldiers were gathering for dinner when Colonel Slough's carriage returned. The men let up a spontaneous cheer as it passed them. The Colonel blinked and touched the rim of his hat, but passed by without saying a word.

"What is wrong with him?" George asked.

Luther snorted. "Here we go and show our loyalty and support and what do we get back? Not so much as a by-your-leave! He's one stuck-up son of a biscuit eater. And he waited for us to break the trail and tamp down the snow so's he'd have himself a nice, smooth ride."

Cian watched the carriage disappear into the darkness beyond the fires. Colonel Slough may have come from an illustrious family. He may have been a lawyer and an assemblyman back in Ohio, but he was no born leader. Not like Major Chivington. As Cian crawled into his blankets that evening, he considered what made the one man so beloved while the other was not. He resolved to become a leader like John Chivington.

Before sunrise the next morning, a train of mule-drawn, flat-bed ambulances rumbled into camp carrying severely wounded men who'd been evacuated from Fort Union. Word traveled back through the ranks who'd crowded around, eager for news. Fort Union, which lay just 120 miles south of them, remained in Union hands, and all reports indicated that the Confederate Army was still in Santa Fe. But the 400 regular soldiers and 400 volunteers wouldn't be able to hold Fort Union alone. The reinforcements from Colorado must reach the fort before the rebels did.

Again, Major Chivington climbed onto a packing crate and gave a rousing speech. This time, he asked every man who was willing to make a forced march for the right to save Fort Union to step two paces forward. As far as Cian could tell, every man did.

The infantry left their backpacks with a corporal's guard. They emptied the wagons and headed off, marching when they could and riding in the wagons when they were too exhausted to continue. The cavalry, which included Samuel Cook's men, were to ride ahead. Cian mounted Henrietta for the first time since they'd gone through the pass.

The plains stretched out, a vast sea of grass with whitecaps of snow. Cian remembered clutching the railings as he stood between his parents on the ship that brought them from Ireland to Boston in 1847. They'd been so hopeful, the vast and barren sea a future they could fill with whatever they wanted. Now both Mam and Da were gone. The future looked bleak and threatening. If he could get through this war, he faced a future he could fill with whatever he wanted. But what did he want? To stay in the Army and serve under John Chivington? To go back to mining? Or was there something else? Cian swallowed hard and let Henrietta find her place among the other mounts. He would worry about the future when it arrived.

They rode all day through strong wind and blowing snow. At nightfall, they came to Reyado, a settlement built beside a small creek. Reyado had a central plaza surrounded by tall adobe walls that helped shield the Army from the winds. Set around the plaza were houses, each with its own courtyard. Someone guided the cavalry to an adobe-walled corral where they could pull the saddles off their tired mounts.

"Nice place," Cian said to E.D. as they were brushing down their mounts.

"I hear tell this is Kit Carson's old place," Sam Cook said. "Him and Lucien Maxwell used to be neighbors here."

"Kit Carson? *The* Kit Carson?" Cian asked.

Sam nodded. "There's only one Kit Carson."

"Where's he now?" Cian looked around as if he expected the famous mountain man to stride out from behind a wall.

Sam shrugged. "I hear he lives in Taos now. But Kit joined up, just like us when the war started, so he's probably not sitting around his *hacienda*. Maxwell's still here, though: one of the biggest honchos around these parts. He stands to lose a lot if the Rebs come through here, so he can be generous."

"Generous like how?" Cian asked.

"Generous like this." George staggered up to them, an immense bag cradled in his arms. "We're getting a pound of beef for each man. 160 pounds of sugar and 100 pounds of coffee, too, and this here's oats for the horses. Get a fire going and cook up yer meat. We pull out early."

While E.D. wandered down to the stream to find saplings to use as meat skewers, Cian fought to start a campfire. Wind whirled around the plaza, which filled with smoke and flying ash. The men sat, turning their spits of meat and cursing the wind.

"I prefer my meat seasoned with pepper, not peppered with ashes," Luther grumbled as he wiped away a smoky tear.

"Least we got meat," George said, testing a piece with his finger.

"Eat while you can, boys. Then find someplace to get some sleep. Me and the other officers are meeting in Maxwell's house to discuss strategy," Sam said as he climbed to his feet. Cian stuffed the last of his meat into his mouth and followed the others to the barn, where they could sleep out of the wind for at least a few hours.

"I heard that Chivington gave up his horse to pull one of the wagons today," Luther said as they bedded down.

"The big gray one? He is a beauty," George said.

"He's a dead beauty now," Luther added. "His heart couldn't take the constant strain. Neither could the saddle mule Chivington switched to."

"We lost a lot of mounts today," E.D. added. "This ride's just too hard for them."

"That's why Sam traded his in," Luther said. "Rode over to one of those ranches we passed, and chose a new mount."

E.D. raised one eyebrow. "He stole it?"

"Nope," Luther said. "Requisitioned it. You can bet the Rebs have been doing the same thing all the way up the Rio Grande."

Whoever was doing it—Confederate or Union—it was still stealing, Cian thought. He remembered how many times he'd pilfered an apple or a sausage hanging in a vendor's stall back when he was a starving waif in Boston. He hadn't felt the least sorry for his actions back then. He'd done what he had to, to survive. But now, after being with E.D., he wondered if all this requisitioning was right. He hoped the Confederates would break and run all the way back to Texas soon. Then he and his friends could return to Colorado, and the New Mexicans could have their land back. If he were a New Mexican, that's what he would want: To have his land left in peace.

CHAPTER TWENTY-THREE
LAND OF MILK AND HONEY

Jemmy Martin
San Antonito
March 12, 1862

Jemmy and Willie joined the long line of men and wagons that left Tijeras. They walked behind the lumbering medical wagon, their hands stuffed into their pockets and their heads down. The road traveled north up a little valley, rising as it followed an icy stream that burbled along, sparking in the sunshine. On their left, the mountain that separated them from the Rio Grande Valley rose in a constant slope through pine forests. On their right, a rocky ridge cut off their view to the east.

"Those lucky stiffs what got sent back to Albuquerque

get to go north along the river," a soldier near Jemmy said.

An older soldier snorted, then spit a brown stream of tobacco before replying. "Ye ain't been in this country afore, has ye? I was with the dragoons before this war started. I been between Santa Fe and Albuquerque by both routes. This here's the easier one."

"You're kidding. Through the mountains is easier?" the younger soldier asked.

"Yep. Going up the Rio means fighting through sand and over about a hunnert rolling hills. And then you get to what they call La Bajada. That's Mexican for 'the place you go down,' only you go up it. An' that's where it gets really rough."

Jemmy shook his head. Sibley's Army of New Mexico had entered the territory in one long and proud column. Now the lack of food and fodder had forced the army to separate and separate again. Now, they were spread thin over a hundred miles. It was like taking a full glass of water and turning it over: the column spread out until the land swallowed it. Without the strength of numbers, would the individual men ever make it back to Texas?

They passed a mountain village with an adobe church, a cluster of flat-roofed houses, and a pond hidden among a stand of cottonwood trees. Jemmy didn't see any signs of life. No people. No cows. No goats, or chickens, or ducks. Jemmy turned his gaze to the hills, wondering where the villagers had hidden themselves.

An hour later, the road bent over the top of a hill and flowed down the other side, into another empty village. They passed a house behind which bees lazily buzzed around half a dozen wicker cones. Jemmy watched the front of the column pull off into a field just across from the church.

"I think we're done walking," Jemmy said.

"That's good. I don't feel so good," Willie answered.

It suddenly occurred to Jemmy that Willie, who'd jabbered all the way from Socorro, had been silent the better part of an hour. He looked down at the drummer boy. Willie's cheeks were flushed, two red patches blazing on his pale face. "You don't look so good, either. Let me feel yer forehead. Yer burning up!"

Willie rubbed a hand across his chest. "An' I feel sore here. Like the sand in my socks, but when I breathe."

Jemmy put his ear to Willie's chest. The boy's breath rumbled in and out of him. Jemmy felt panic rising in his throat, threatening to cut off his breathing. He'd lost William Kemp to pneumonia on the road to Fort Craig. He couldn't lose Willie, too. "Hey, Thomas," Jemmy called. You got any *pulveris licii* in that wagon?"

Thomas stopped rooting around in the supplies and looked up. "Any what?"

"*Pulveris licii*. It's a syrup that smells like licorice."

Thomas scratched his head. "And you know this because?"

"Because doc gave me some, back before the battle at Valverde Ford, for a friend of mine what had pneumonie."

Thomas shook his head and went back to rummaging through the supplies. "And you still remember its name? Maybe you should be in charge here. But no, far's I know, it got used up long before we got to Socorro."

Jemmy nodded. He felt himself slump with disappointment. What was he going to do? An idea came to him. He turned back to Willie and set a hand on the drummer boy's shoulder. "You climb up in the back of the wagon. Tell Thomas you need some rest. I saw something a little while back I gotta go back for."

Jemmy walked back to the wicker cones at the bottom of the hill. He was right; they were beehives. Jemmy knocked on the door to the closest house. No one answered. Was this house as empty as it appeared to be? Had the inhabitants taken their pigs and chickens and escaped into the hills? Jemmy thrust his hand into his pocket.

"*Por favor*," he said loudly, trying hard to remember what little Spanish he'd learned from Arsenio and Fungillo, "*yo* need *socorro. Por mi* little *compadre.*"

Jemmy stood still, listening. He felt color rise in his cheeks. Was he talking to himself? Half-sure he was making no sense, half-hoping he was, and continued, "*Yo soy Americano dinero.*"

Someone inside the house laughed. Jemmy's hopes rose.

"*Yo soy no mucho*, but *yo* will give *todo a tu.*"

The door opened a crack. An elderly woman, her head wrapped in a shawl, frowned out at him. She was so old that Jemmy wondered if she had been abandoned when the rest of the household fled to the hills. Was she so old as to be feeble minded? He spoke quickly before the woman could slam the door in his face. "*Yo's compadre es* sick. *Yo* need some honey *por* him. *Yo* can pay you *esto.*" Jemmy reached into his pocket. He pulled out the half-dime that Raul had given him and held it up between his finger and thumb.

The woman raised her eyebrows and clutched the shawl even tighter beneath her chin.

"*Por* honey. From the bees."

The woman's eyebrows raised even higher.

Jemmy sighed. "I guess I gots to show you." He pointed at the beehives, then stuck his hands in his armpits. Flapping his elbows up and down, he walked around in a circle making a buzzing noise.

The woman smiled at him. "Young man, your Spanish is atrocious," she said.

Jemmy's eyebrows rose. "You speak American?"

"I speak English, young man. And French. And Spanish. We New Mexicans are not the uneducated peasants you think we are."

Jemmy nodded. "I am sorry, *Señora*. And I don't aim to be offensive. If'n anyone's an uneducated hick, it's me. But I have this friend. A boy, really, and he's sick and I'll do anything to get some honey to help him. My ma used to give us honey in hot water, with a little whiskey when me or my brother was ailing."

The woman held out her hand. Jemmy dropped the half-dime into the woman's palm. The door closed. Jemmy waited, staring at the door of the silent house and wondering if the woman was coming back. After a moment, the door opened and the woman held out a clay jar.

"*Miel,*" she said. Jemmy pulled off the lid, dipped a finger into the sticky golden substance, stuck his finger in his mouth, and smiled.

"*Sí. Miel. Gracias,*" he answered, then added "Delicioso," which may or may not have been Spanish. The smile on the woman's face told him that she understood. Or, she was laughing at him.

"And here is your change," the woman said, dropping two pennies into Jemmy's hand.

That evening, Jemmy tucked Willie up against him as they stared into the fire. Willie sipped the hot water, whiskey, and honey potion that Jemmy had made after trading his pennies for whiskey. The sun had dropped behind the hill, but the sky was still clear and light. Evening could last a long time up in the hills.

"I think it's just a cold," Willie said. "I's feeling much better."

"That's good," Jemmy answered, and smiled as he remembered the woman's quizzical expression as he danced around, trying to imitate a bee.

CHAPTER TWENTY-FOUR
HURRY UP AND WAIT

Cian Lochlann
Outside Fort Union
March 11, 1862

Luther Wilson speared a hunk of meat with his fork, brought it to his face, and squinted at it. With a snort, he flung it back into the stewpot. "Know what I love about this infernal army!? It is all hurry up and wait. Key, when will this meat be cooked?"

"'Tis done when 'tis done, and the army shall move us when they move us. I cannot be predicting either," Cian answered.

"I don't see why we had to endure a ninety-mile forced march just to sit around here and wait," George said. "Wouldn't have killed off so many horses had we taken it slower."

Cian nodded. When Captain Cook's Company F had arrived at Fort Union just after dawn, they'd expected to be welcomed as heroes. Instead, they were told to wait outside the fort until the infantry arrived. Apparently, entering together in a grand parade was more important than watering the weary horses. "Good thing we drug this meat all the way from Reyado. Otherwise, we'd have no breakfast. I don't 'spect they'd want skeletons in their parade. How far behind is the infantry, anyway?"

Wilson squinted into the north. "Hours, I expect. I hope they're here by lunch. There's not enough meat here to tide us over longer than that."

After the meat had been eaten, Cian walked around what was reported to be the best fort in the west. Fort Union sat on the western side of a wide, smooth valley that had a little stream running through it. An earlier Fort Union, now used as an arsenal, stood a little farther to the west, closer to a mesa that might have enabled enemies to fire down into the fort. The newer fort, whose revetments were still incomplete, was supposedly unbreachable and bomb-proof. Cian drew his knife and carved his initials into the wall as easily as if it were chalk. How could a fort made of adobe, brick made from sun-dried mud, withstand a cannonade?

The infantry did not arrive in time for Luther Wilson to get lunch inside the fort. They finally staggered in as the sun dipped behind the western mountains. To the tattoo of drums, the Colorado Volunteers formed into columns and marched, colors flying, through the gate. They halted in the parade grounds, where they stood at attention and listened to speeches by both Colonel Paul, the commander of the fort, and New Mexico Territorial Governor Henry

Connelly. Darkness fell, and the speeches went on. Neither man mentioned either Valverde or the Confederates, which made the bone-weary marchers even more irritable. Finally, the men were dismissed. Cian followed George and Luther to the fort's kitchens.

"When's dinner?" George asked a private who was scrubbing out a large pot.

The man looked up, a confused look on his face. "Two hours ago."

"But, what about us?" George sounded like a child who'd missed his nap. "We were still waiting outside the gate two hours ago."

The pot-washer set down his rag and leaned against one of the prep tables. "Colonel Slough told Colonel Paul that his men were all old mountaineers and accustomed to hardships. Therefore, no orders for food or quarters were necessary. If you are as tough as your commander says, go find your own eats and your own place to sleep."

Cian felt his face flush. He balled up his fists and lunged at the man, but E.D. grabbed him by the scruff of the neck and hauled him back. "Let it go, Key," he muttered under his breath.

"If we learned one thing at Camp Weld, it was procurement techniques," Luther said as they skulked away. "We can apply them now, since our commander has not seen fit to do it for us."

"Not me," E.D. said. "I'll find some rations elsewhere." E.D. gave Cian one more shake, then let him go.

Cian glared at E.D. "Stop being so sanctimonious! They made us practically run all the way here from the Colorado border, then had us cool our heels outside while they ate. We deserve better than that!"

"Sometimes what one deserves is not what one gets." E.D. turned and walked toward the tents. Cian glared at his back, his blood still coursing hot at the insult of it all. Finally, he turned and followed Luther and the others to Robber's Row, the area where the sutlers set up their stores. All were closed for the night. Luther stopped in front of the most prosperous looking shop. He put a finger to his lips and looked around to be sure that no one was looking. "George, I think this door could use an application of your shoulder."

George smiled. "Your druthers is my ruthers." George leaned into the door, which splintered so quickly that he found himself on the floor.

"Everybody grab something! We'll reconnoiter at the corrals," Luther said as the men burst through the splintered door. Cian grabbed a big wheel of cheese. He was about to scurry away when he noticed George curled up in a ball on the floor, his arms protecting his head.

"What are you doing?" Cian asked.

"Keeping my noggin from getting stove in," George answered.

"Well, the men're gone now, and if you don't skedaddle, the guard'll arrest you when they respond to all the noise, and you'll end up in the brig." Cian helped George to his feet, and the two slipped into the darkness. Back at the corral, they found everyone hunched down and quiet.

"And there's Key and Nelson," Luther said. "That's all of us, present and accounted for. So, what do we have?"

"Champagne," one man said, holding up a wooden crate.

"Me, too," another said.

"Crackers," a third man said, holding up his crate.

"And I have cheese to go with them," Cian said.

"And canned peaches for dessert!" another man said.

"Good job foraging, men," Luther said. "Let's have us a feast, courtesy the sutlers of Fort Union. When we're done, I want George and Key to scatter the empty cases and tins near the tents of sleeping regulars, so they'll be blamed for the theft, not us."

* * *

The next morning, Cian awoke in the corral with a splitting headache. He groaned, pressing his palms into the side of his head.

"I daresay your headache's well earned," E.D. said with a chuckle.

"And by that, you mean?"

"You were so drunk last night that I had to go with you when you and George scattered the evidence of your marauding. I practically carried you back and put you to bed."

Cian squeezed his eyes tight. "It wasn't my finest moment," he admitted.

"I thought the Fighting Parson had made you see the light," E.D. said. "You rode all that way in a snowstorm to impress him. You think he'd be impressed by your behavior last night?"

"You're right. He wouldn't." Cian sighed and rubbed a hand over his face. "Ever since me Mam died, I've been slipping into chicanery. And since me Da died, I've had no one to grab me by the collar and haul me back."

E.D. nodded. "So, she was your moral compass and he was your leash?"

"Right. And without them, who's to stop me?"

"You are," E.D. said.

Cian's eyes flew open. "You don't understand. I've been desperate. Near to starving and freezing to death."

"Any nearer than I have been these last weeks?"

The silenced stretched as the question hung in the air between them. Cian wanted to leap to his feet and shout that E.D. was being high-handed. But his legs shook too much for him to leap up, and his head would split if he tried to shout. And anyways, E.D. was right. Cian had to admit to himself that he was his own worst enemy. His temper and impetuousness was not going to get him the life that he wanted.

"Here. Maybe this will help." E.D. held a steaming mug of coffee beneath Cian's nose.

"Thanks," Cian said, "for the coffee, and for the straight talk. I t'ink I need both. And a friend like you to give it to me."

Three days after the Colorado volunteers arrived at Fort Union, 150 rebel prisoners from an intercepted supply train were brought to the fort. All of Cook's men went out to see them come in. Cian had expected the prisoners to shuffle in, their heads down in shame. Instead, they sauntered in, shoulders squared.

"Enjoy yourselves now! Y'all are going to be in a world a hurt real soon!" one of the rebels yelled.

"Them New Mexicans is rushing to join us! Sibley's ranks're swelling with 'em," another shouted.

"And they're all going to whoop yer sorry arses," a third added.

Cian saw red. He would have jumped into the middle of the prisoners, fists flying, had Luther not held him back. "The time for fighting is coming, but it's not now. Get yourself locked in the stockade, and you'll miss it."

Cian shrugged out of Luther's grasp, but his eyes fell on where E.D. stood by, his arms crossed over his chest and a scowl on his face. Cian shook himself, letting his anger drain into the ground at his feet. "T'anks, Luther. I'll do you proud when the time comes. You'll see."

Finally, on the afternoon of March 21, Samuel Cook appeared in the middle of his men's encampment. "Well, boys," he said, taking off his hat and mopping his forehead. "This is it. The Colonel just issued orders."

George scratched his head. "Which Colonel, Sam? There are so many of them, I get confused."

Sam scowled at George. "Slough, Sergeant. We are marching south tomorrow to engage the enemy. And do not call me Sam."

George scrambled to his feet. "Yes, sir, Captain Cook! I shall rally the men and have them ready to ride tomorrow, with boots blackened and polished!"

While George bellowed orders, Cian found Henrietta in the corral. He brushed her down, picked rocks and weeds from her hooves and gave her a pep talk about the ride ahead. To his surprise, the hinny had become like family to him. Cian had never been attached to an animal before. His family had been too poor to even own a dog. Was learning to love and care for Henrietta part of his redemption?

"Boys," Luther Wilson said that evening as they sat around the fire, "this being possibly our last night before the fight, I believe a last fling is in order. Anyone want to go on another procurement raid to Robber's Row this evening?"

"Not me," E.D. said. "I have some reading to do."

Cian looked up. He took in a hesitant breath. "Me, neither. We got a long ride tomorrow. I t'ink I shall turn in early."

Luther lifted an eyebrow. "You going soft and sanctimonious on us, Key?"

George scrambled to his feet. "Let's get going."

As the rest of the men followed Luther into the dark, E.D. and Cian threw another few sticks on the fire and rolled out their bedrolls in its warm glow.

"Glad you stayed with me," E.D. said.

"Me, too," Cian replied. "I t'ink you were right about Chivington not wanting me around if I be one of the rowdy ones. I been t'inking. I've only signed on for this campaign as a volunteer, but if he'll have me, I'll sign up for regular army, and be a runner and aide for the Major. T'is a good way to be fed and sheltered."

"You're thinking that Major Chivington can be your moral compass and your guide?" E.D. asked.

"That's it," Cian answered.

"What's that your Ma used to say? Thinking is believing? I think you've found something to believe in," E.D. said.

Cian gazed into the dancing fire. He felt as if the path had been laid out for him. Now, all he had to do was follow it. "And you, E.D.? You still planning on buying that farm after we lick these Confederates and send them back to Texas?"

"Yup," E.D. said. "And I'm going to marry a good woman who'll bake bread and pies and mend my shirts. I'm going to have a lot of kids, and in the evening, they'll sit at my feet and I'll read *Robinson Crusoe* to them."

"Mam and Da used to read to me in the evenings, by the stove. Those were happy times," Cian said. He felt a nostalgia swell within his heart until it became an ache for the future. He drifted off to sleep and dreamed of himself sitting in an upholstered chair in front of a warm stove, a book on his lap and a captain's bars on his shoulders.

The next morning, the column proceeded south, the mountains on their right growing in size as they traveled. Late on the third day, Sam Cook rode back from an officer's meeting. "Ready for some action?" he asked. "Sixty of the best men from Companies A, D, and E are being loaded into wagons so that they can be pushed forward quickly. Company F is going to ride escort."

"Pushed forward quickly for what?" E.D.'s voice sounded tight in his throat.

"To be a vanguard, Major Chivington in command. The plan is to make a sudden dash to Santa Fe and capture or defeat the enemy before they can move on Fort Union."

"Now we're talking!" George responded. "Let me round up the troops!"

"George." Cook cut off George mid-way through his bellow. "You do not have to round them up. They are all here. Just pull them out of the line and have them follow me to the front of the column."

The vanguard rode hard through the day as the path before them rose up into rolling foothills. Soon they were surrounded by piñons and ponderosa pines. The trail turned west, into the Sangre de Cristo mountains just as the sun set, casting crimson linings on the clouds.

"That's appropriate," E.D. said, pointing at the sky. "In a place named after the blood of Christ, it's fitting that even the sky should appear bloody." The farther they rode, the quieter and more circumspect E.D. became. Cian noticed that the others grew rowdier, anticipating the fight ahead.

"E.D.? Are you all right?" Cian asked.

E.D. shrugged. "We're all thinking about blood, both ours and the enemy's. But I can't help feeling fatalistic."

Cian reached over and punched his friend in the arm. "The sooner we beat the rebels, the sooner you'll be back in Burlington. Sitting on the porch of your homestead."

It was closing in on midnight when the Major called a halt to the column, announcing that they had reached a ranch owned by a Union supporter. The ranch had an excellent spring, and good, flat ground on which to bivouac. Cian slid off Henrietta's back and gave her a pat. He walked her to the corral and made sure that she was watered and fed before he found a place to roll out his bedroll. He was asleep before his head hit the ground.

Cian awoke just before dawn. He rose and walked into the brush to relieve himself, looking at the land that had been enshrouded in darkness when he arrived the night before. They had camped in the front yard of a ranch that had several flat-roofed, one-story buildings, all of which were made of adobe, the same mixture of mud and straw that Fort Union had been constructed from. Cian walked through the compound, sizing it up. One building looked to be living quarters. Through an open door, he saw a woman working in a kitchen. A sign over the door of a building with a whitewashed veranda running along the front announced that it was a trading post. Another had a sign indicating a tavern. There were also grain bins, some stables, and the corrals which held the Union horses. A creek ran past the buildings.

Curious, Cian opened the door to one small building and stepped inside to find it was just a storage shed for horse gear. A heap of saddle blankets lay in one corner, and tangled reins and bits hung from pegs in the walls. Cian ran his fingernail across the wall, scraping off some of the adobe, just as he had at Fort Union. It was a marvel that these buildings had not dissolved into mounds of mud, he thought. New Mexico must not get anywhere near as much rain as Colorado did.

"Having fun sightseeing?" E.D. asked with a grin and approached his friend. "Come on. I've got someone I want you to meet."

"And who would that be?" Cian tipped his head, but his friend just smiled. E.D. led them to the house, where the woman was still working in the kitchen. A long line of soldiers stood at the door with their plates in their hands.

"Ellene, this is the soldier I was telling you about. Key, meet Mrs. Kozlowski. She and her husband own this ranch."

The woman who looked away from the frying pan had dark hair and dark eyes that twinkled merrily at him. Her cheeks were reddened from the heat of the stove. Cian blinked hard. Was he awake or was this a dream? Mrs. Kozlowski looked so much like his own Mam that he had to hold back tears. He took off his hat and held it respectfully at his chest. "I'll be pleased to be making your acquaintance, ma'am."

She smiled at him. "And I'll be pleased to be meeting someone whose voice sounds like home. Now be giving me your plate so I can put your breakfast on it."

Cian stared, his mouth agape. "You're from County Kerry?"

She nodded. "Grew up in MacGillycuddy's Reeks, same as you if I hear your accent right. Now then; where's the plate?" When Cian didn't move, she laughed, pulled two plates off a shelf and loaded them each with fried trout, a spoonful of beans, and a biscuit. She handed the plates to Cian and E.D.. "Get moving. There's plenty of hungry men behind you."

E.D. took Cian by the elbow and turned him around. Before they got to the door, a dark-haired little man with a beard running along his jaw came in holding up a string of trout. "Here are more for the frying pan, El. And I have a half dozen boys with their hooks in the stream. We will soon have them all fed."

"That was Mr. Kozlowski," E.D. said as he guided Cian into the yard and rifled through his rucksack to find them forks.

"Jaysus! She looks just like me Mam," Cian said.

E.D. looked up. "Who? Oh! Kozlowski's wife! I did not know your mother looked like that, but I thought you should meet her because she sounds just like you. These people run a nice place. Four or five little Kozlowski's running about. Reminds me of home."

Cian nodded, then stuffed his mouth with beans. There were Irish all over the place. Some, even, in Samuel Cook's company. But no one had looked or sounded as much like his Mam as this woman did. Maybe it was a sign that he was finally on the road to redemption. He'd been angry with the world since Mam died. Now, with E.D.'s help, Cian was regaining his old self. For the first time in a long while, he felt at peace and was willing to work hard and fairly. Cian looked up when a shadow fell on him. It was George, standing straight, tall, and proud. With the rising sun at his back, he looked like an angel haloed in light.

"I just got an assignment! Me! My mother will be so proud! Chivington says I am to gather up twenty men and ride reconnaissance late tonight. We are to scout between here and some ranch where they raise pigeons, see if we can find any Rebels. You two want to be part of the twenty?"

Cian shoveled in another spoonful of beans, then nodded. This, too, must be part of that road to redemption.

CHAPTER TWENTY-FIVE
OPENING THE BALL

Cian Lochlann
Glorieta Pass
March 26, 1862

George Nelson and his twenty men saddled up and rode out of Kozlowski's Ranch at two in the morning. While many were from Colorado, Nelson had also picked a few New Mexico Volunteers who knew the lay of the land a little better. Some had even fought at Valverde, then been sent north on a roundabout route by Colonel Canby.

"This ranch we are to reconnoiter," E.D. babbled, "it is not a ranch where they raise pigeons. I checked with Kozlowski. It is a ranch owned by a pigeon. At least, that is what they call him. He is not a pigeon, but a Frenchman, and his real name is Valle. Alexander Valle. Only that is not his real name, either. His real name is French, but the locals call him Valle because his ranch is in the valley."

"And where in the Sam Hill did you learn all that? Chivington told me none of it, and this is supposed to be my mission," George said with a grumble.

"I was talking with Kozlowski, and he told me! Did you know that there are only three men in the Pecos area who aren't Mexicans? Kozlowski, and Pigeon, and one more, a real American. Think on that! One English speaking American in the whole area! This is just like being in a foreign country here!" E.D. took in a big breath, then continued. "Pigeon is called Pigeon because he holds lots of fandangos up at his place, and he struts around like a pigeon. Dances like one, too, flapping his wings."

"Speaking of flapping," George said, "you think we will surprise any Confederates with you flapping your gums that way?"

"Sorry," E.D. whispered.

Cian pulled Henrietta up to E.D.'s much taller buckskin gelding. He reached up and slugged his friend in the arm encouragingly. "Nervous?"

"I guess," E.D. answered in a low voice. Cian saw his friend's shoulder hunch as if he were avoiding getting wet in a rainstorm.

"We're a nervous and excited lot," Cian said. "You, you're normally reserved. Now you're babbling like a brook. And George, who's usually so amiable, is taking this assignment far too seriously."

"The prospect of running into the enemy is making me jittery," E.D. admitted. "Every bush looks like a rebel hunched over, ready to fire. Every bat that skitters by sounds like a volley of musket fire whistling overhead."

"Eight months of drilling and gun practice, learning

to ride and recognize drum tattoos and bugle signals, all leading up to a battle. Hard to believe we were impatient for it," Cian said.

"Most of these men have been chewing at the bit to 'see the elephant.' Now, I wonder if 'the elephant' is too big for us to handle," E.D. said.

"We're ready," Cian assured him, "even if we don't t'ink so."

Kozlowski's ranch occupied the broad valley where Glorieta Creek met the Pecos River. As they traveled east up the creek, the valley narrowed and the steep canyon walls on either side loomed ever higher. The men were forced to slow their pace to a crawl, their mounts plodding along the ravine. Not much moonlight made it into the canyon and through the tall pines. It was clear that the sun didn't make it into this canyon by day, either. Crusty snow, trampled into mush and refrozen in the cold night air, made the footing difficult for the horses, whose hooves crunched through it more loudly than Cian would have liked. At times they lost the trail and rode through the trees, but there was no real way to get lost. Even in this darkness, the narrowness of the canyon and the gradual rise of the land away from Kozlowski's ranch made the way clear. Each time they lost the trail, it crossed their path again before they had time to worry.

They reached a ranch as the sky was lightening, the stars fading into the gray. Here, the valley had narrowed so much that the ranch took the entire valley floor. There was only room for the buildings, corrals, and the trail between the narrow canyon walls on the south and slopes of tall pines, piñon, and juniper thickets to the north. Beyond the ranch, the valley widened a little, a heavily wooded ridge running down its center.

A man stood on the front porch, as if waiting for them.

He was short and dark haired, and Cian assumed that he was Mexican until he spoke. Cian could not identify the accent. Might it be French?

"Identify yourselves," the man shouted.

George stopped his men at the fence line and had them draw their pistols before he answered gravely, with a formality that Cian had not heard from him before. Clearly, he was taking this assignment very seriously. "We are advance scouts of the Colorado First Volunteers, sent out by Major John Chivington to probe for the enemy. Have you seen any? Or are you, sir, a Rebel?"

The man danced with delight, flapping his elbows and clicking his heels against the porch's floorboards. Instantly, Cian knew that this must be the man they called Pigeon. "The miners from Pike's Peak! You are just the men I have been waiting for! I was told you were on your way! Yes, four mounted brigands came through here just a few hours ago! They were asking if I had seen you, my friends! They headed east, where you just came from. You did not see them? Perhaps, in the darkness, you passed each other?"

Pigeon gesticulated back the way George's men had come, so George turned his troop around and they headed back on the Santa Fe trail. They had not gone more than a mile when they saw four men up ahead.

"Are you here to relieve us?" one of the men called.

Quickly, George waved his hand. The Coloradans surrounded the four riders and drew their guns. "Yes," George said. "We came to relieve you of your arms."

Cian let out a sigh of relief when the four raised their hands, surrendering without resistance.

"You look familiar," one of the New Mexico Volunteers said. "Were you on Colonel Canby's staff, down at Fort Craig?"

The Confederate nodded. "I was. Deserted right after the battle for Valverde Ford."

"I heard about you," a Coloradan said contemptuously. "You're McIntire. We don't like traitors."

"And you," another of the Coloradans pointed at another of the four men. "Aren't you H.H. Hall? Did I not play poker with you in Denver?"

"I am," the man said.

Cian let out a low whistle. Confederate Captain H.H. Hall was well known in Denver. He'd been arrested there, but escaped jail and rode south. Now George had captured him and the notorious turncoat Lieutenant John McIntire without having to fire a single shot. "Your Ma's going to be mighty proud of you when we write to her about this, George."

"Don't that beat all? My mother is going to bust the buttons on her petticoats, she'll be so proud," George answered. His smile glowed brighter than the rising sun.

* * *

By eight in the morning, the four Confederates were locked away in a room in Kozlowski's Inn. Cian had helped lead the men into the room, and he had studied the room carefully, wondering if it would do. Like most of the structures he had seen in New Mexico, it was made of adobe bricks. Cian still wasn't sure if bricks made from sun-dried mud were strong, but there was no time to test the walls nor question their integrity. He made sure that a sturdy crossbar held the door in place, then left to join John Chivington, who was leading a force of over four hundred men towards Pigeon's Ranch.

Pickets led the way, with the infantry marching behind them and the cavalry riding in the rear. They passed the ruins of the old Pecos pueblo and turned into the valley that rose ever upward, becoming narrower until it reached the summit at Glorieta Pass. At noon they stopped and ate lunch at the ranch, while Pigeon animatedly told them about what lay ahead. They gained the summit and were heading south, down into Apache Canyon, when the advance scouts came charging back, hauling Confederate prisoners.

"Sir!" one of them shouted, saluting Chivington, "The enemy is just ahead! Give 'em hell, boys! Hurrah for the Pike's Peakers!"

Cian watched the infantry strip for the encounter that they knew was coming. Knapsacks, canteens, and over-coats flew through the air, landing in bushes and under-foot. The men flung aside anything that wasn't essential. The ranks closed in. They rushed forward on the double quick. Cian's heart pounded in his ears. His hands grew slick with perspiration. He glanced aside and saw the look of steely determination on E.D.'s face. It gave him courage.

Around a bend in the road, a treeless meadow opened in front of them. Not two hundred yards ahead, a full company of mounted men faced them. One man carried a red flag with a single white star. Cian pulled back on his reins. His heart pounded. Two howitzers pointed directly at him.

"Take cover!" someone yelled just as flashes of flame erupted from the howitzers. Cian tried to control Henrietta as the canister shot soared harmlessly over his head.

A cloud of smoke rolled away from the barrel. Cian watched the infantry in front of him jerk, then bunch into tight groups. The cavalry horses plunged about, whin-nying in their terror and creating tumultuous confusion. Everyone shouted at once.

Sam Cook screamed. Blood streamed down his leg.

"He's been hit! Sam's been hit!" Cian shouted, but no one was listening. Everyone was trying to control their mounts.

A frowning Major Chivington appeared through the smoke and chaos, shouting commands and demanding attention like Cian figured no one had since Moses led his people through the Red Sea. "Captain Cook! Take your men and fall back until they can get their mounts under control. Infantry! Split in two and go up the sides of the pass! You can catch the Rebels in your crossfire!"

"Yes, sir!" someone in the Infantry shouted.

"Yes, sir! Men, to me!" Sam Cook shouted. Cian and the rest of Company F rode back through the lines, their mounts calming as they made distance between themselves and the guns.

Cian rode to the cluster of horsemen around Sam, who was telling everyone and no one in particular about his wound. "It did not even hurt. A little sting, was all. I thought it was a wasp until I slapped at it and my hand came away red with blood."

The neat, round hole in Cook's right thigh made Cian's vision blur. His heart pounded. He clutched at his reins and hoped he wouldn't pass out.

E.D. climbed off his big bay horse, pulled off his neckerchief and tied it tightly around the hole in Sam's leg. "I figure that makes you the first known casualty of the Battle, Captain Cook, sir. Congratulations," E.D. said as calmly as if they were at home. "You shall get a mention in the official record. George, give Sam a swig of whisky to take a little off the shock."

Almost immediately, half-dozen men shouted George's name. George fumbled in his saddlebags until he found his canteen. Sam may have taken the first drink, but a lot of men followed. Away from the shooting, the horses calmed. The men sat in the saddles and watched the battle.

"Lookie that one," George said. "He's in line with the

Texans, but he's wearing a Federal overcoat."

"Probably either captured at Valverde or pillaged from a Federal supply depot," William Marshall answered. "Keep that in mind, men. Don't assume that anyone in blue is on our side."

"Look at our men up on the high ground on both sides of the canyon. It's like shooting fish in a barrel," Luther Wilson said, laughing. The men of Company F let up a loud cheer as the Confederate center appeared to pull back. The Union forces filled the gap. The Confederates backed down Apache Canyon. Company F trailed behind. Foot by foot, both armies moved west through the canyon. Finally, after they'd moved about a mile and a half, the Confederates reformed a defensive line between two steep canyon walls. Behind them, the canyon opened into a flat, boulder-strewn, treeless glen that Cian guessed to be 250 yards wide and 600 yards long. A deep *arroyo*, a dry riverbed, crossed the glen. The only way across it was a narrow wooden bridge.

Everything, it seemed to Cian, depended on the bridge. If the Confederates crossed it, they could pick off Union soldiers as they tried to follow. Union sharpshooters scrambled up the canyon sides, but they couldn't pick off the Rebels who had already crossed and provided a heavy covering fire for their comrades on this side. Slowly, one or two men at a time, the Confederates gained the far side.

George Nelson threw up his hands. "What are we doing, sitting here?"

"Sergeant, have you heard an order for us to do anything else?" Sam Cook snapped. "We'll go when we're ordered to go. If the Major wants to hold us in reserve, so be it."

The last of the Rebels crossed the bridge. The crackle

of rifles slowed to an occasional pop. Cian watched the Confederates throw off their backpacks and lay down, laughing in relief. They were at a stalemate, the yawning *arroyo* an impassable barrier between the two armies. Cian squeezed his fists tight, crushing the reins until they bit into the palms of his hands. He wanted to lash out at those insolent men who thought themselves safe. Frustration made him tremble.

Major Chivington rode to the front of Cook's men. His face mirrored the anger that Cian felt. "Let us cross and engage the enemy," Chivington shouted.

"Crossing that bridge would be suicide," Sam answered. "Every rebel gun is trained on that bridge."

"Who said anything about using a bridge?" With a great scowl on his face, the Major reached into his saddle bags. He pulled out two pistols and shoved them into his waistband. He pulled out two more and tucked one under each arm. He pulled out two more, cocked them, and pointed them skyward.

"God save our country! God save Colorado!" He bellowed the words, then turned his horse and spurred it forward.

For a split second, Company F watched him, transfixed by the man in full regimentals thundering toward the enemy. Then they surged after him, shouting and shooting as their horses pounded across the rocky canyon floor. Chivington reached the edge of the *arroyo* at a full gallop. His horse leaped the chasm and landed on the other side. The Major's pistols blazed.

Cian leaned forward, giving Henrietta full rein. She was smaller than the other men's horses, but he was sure she was more muscular and had more heart than any of them. If Chivington could leap the *arroyo*, then so could he. The exhilaration of being alive and strong and vital quickened his pulse and made his whole body tingle. Around him, men whooped and shouted. Surrounded by comrades, he and the hinny flew across the expanse and landed on the other side.

"To me, men! To me!" Cian heard Major Chivington shouting. He scanned the battlefield and found him on high ground north of the enemy. Cian turned Henrietta and raced to Chivington as Confederates scrambled to their feet and tried to regain order in their ranks.

"Who will lead the charge?" Chivington called.

Cook answered, shouting, "Forward to the run, march!" They raced through the Confederates in the clearing, shooting and slashing with their sabers. The bridge, now undefended, swarmed with Union troops cheering at the top of their lungs. At the southern edge of the clearing, Company F turned and charged back the way they had come, trampling Texans and breaking up their formations while Union troops swept over the bridge and down the canyon like a hurricane. After Company F's third sweep across the clearing, the enemy turned and ran.

Cian stood in his stirrups and howled like a wolf. Elation unlike anything he had ever felt before coursed through him. He had faced the elephant head on, and he had won! All around him, clusters of men cheered, throwing their caps, and firing shots into the air.

The sun set. Dusk was coming, but the field was theirs! Cian turned Henrietta in a full circle, taking in the spectacle.

He stopped. The joy drained from his veins. Close by, the Captain of Company F and his horse lay still on the ground.

"Sam! Somebody, help! My Captain's down!" Cian rushed to kneel beside Sam Cook. He gently lifted his head. The captain's eyes fluttered open, and Cian let out a puff of relief. He hadn't even realized he was holding his breath.

"It's a soldier's fate; I have tried to do my duty. There are others who probably need attention more than I. See them cared for," Sam said in a weak voice.

"Pretty speech, Sam. Bet you've been practicing it for weeks. Come on, let's get that horse off him and see what the damage is," Luther Wilson said. Cian glanced up and saw Luther and George hovering over him. The three tugged at the dead horse until they freed Sam's trapped leg, then sat him up and patted him down, looking for injuries.

"Looks like a ball went right through your leg and into your horse's heart," Luther said. "George, go find a couple of stretcher bearers to carry Sam back to Pigeon's Ranch. I hear a hospital's been set up there."

"Jaysus! And they say lightning doesn't strike twice in the same place! You've got three buckshot and a ball, all in the right thigh, right where E.D. tied his neckerchief. Don't that beat all, E.D.?" Cian looked up, expecting an answer. He got none.

Where was E.D.?

Cian stood up. Before, he had just seen the celebration. Now, he saw dead and dying men and horses. Some wore Confederate uniforms, some Union, and some a mix of the two or none at all. Cian grabbed the arm of the corporal who was placing Captain Cook on his stretcher. "I'm looking for a man on a tall buckskin horse."

The man glanced up. "One rider on a buckskin went down in the *arroyo* during the charge. Might that be him?"

Cian thought he might faint. He sucked in a breath, staggered over to the arroyo. The body of a large, buckskin horse lay at the bottom, with E.D. beside it. Both were very still.

Cian scrambled willy-nilly down the embankment.

He cradled his friend's head in his hands and watched for E.D.'s eyelids to flutter, as Sam's had.

They didn't.

""T'inkin' is believin'," Cian muttered to himself. "You're alive. You have to be."

A drop of water splashed onto E.D.'s face. Cian realized he was crying. Another tear hit E.D.'s face. E.D. flinched.

He was alive!

Cian noticed George and Luther walking over the bridge beside the two stretcher-bearers carrying Sam. "Luther! Sam! Send another stretcher. E.D. needs help." The two talked, then Luther proceeded on with Sam while George ran back to the battlefield. Soon he returned with two more men, who had tied ropes to a stretcher so that it could be lowered over the side of the bridge.

Carefully, Cian lifted his friend's body onto the stretcher. Although he didn't want to cause his friend pain, he sighed in relief when E.D. groaned. It was another sign of life. Four men hauled E.D. up to the bridge while Cian scrambled back up the side of the *arroyo*. He grabbed the back end of the stretcher, telling the man who had been carrying it to find someone else who needed help.

It was fully dark by the time Cian and the stretcher bearer arrived at Pigeon's Ranch. A man with a white apron looked up as he came into the yard. "Dead over there. Wounded, here." He pointed first at a wall on the side of the compound, then at his feet. Cian was relieved to see more men near the aproned man than by the wall. He set down E.D. gently, then sunk to the ground next to him, emotionally and physically exhausted. The aproned man bent down and looked at E.D. "You brought him in; know where he was shot?"

"Don't know that he was," Cian said. "He and his horse did not make the jump over the *arroyo*."

"Ah," the man said. "I am Doctor Bailey. Let me check for broken bones." Beginning with the top of his head, the doctor ran his hands over E.D., sometimes just using his palms, sometimes probing with his fingers. E.D. winced when the doctor touched his shoulder. He groaned and stiffened when the doctor touched his hips and one of his legs. The doctor slipped off E.D.'s boots and continued to move his hands down to the bottoms of E.D.'s feet, then he sat back on his heels and looked at Cian. "Your friend here has a number of broken bones, but none that are out of place and need setting. He may have broken his hip. There is no way to set that. He may have a concussion. Possibly a broken back. But his organs appear intact. Not much we can do for him but let his body heal. Take him into the house where he'll be warmer. When he wakes, spoon feed him some broth."

Cian nodded, grateful for the hope the doctor offered him. An orderly helped him carry E.D.'s stretcher into Pigeon's tavern and set it on the floor. Cian was about to lay down next to his friend when he saw a Confederate soldier sitting in a chair nearby. Anger rose like bile in his throat. "You! The doctors may be willing to treat you, but that don't mean you deserve a chair! Out of it, now!"

The man didn't move.

Cian grabbed the man by the front of his jacket and gave him a violent shake. The man's head lolled back, his eyes vacant and staring. A pool of blood covered the ground beneath the chair. All Cian's fear, exhaustion and relief surged into an irrational, blind fury. Without thinking, he hauled the man out of the chair and threw him out the door. "You've got no business to be occupying a chair—you're a dead man!" he shouted.

Doctor Bailey, who was bent over another man in the yard, looked up and frowned. "If he's dead, why are you yelling at him?"

Cian realized he was shaking all over. He had no idea why he'd attacked the dead Confederate. It had just happened. He sunk to the ground and buried his face in his hands. "I don't know," he murmured weakly. "I don't know anything."

Doc Bailey sighed. "The shock of the day. Fighting does strange things to a man's psyche. Get some rest. Get some food. You'll feel better. But before you take care of yourself, take care of him." Doctor Bailey stabbed a finger at the dead man lying in a heap. "Pick him up and put him with the others."

Cian grabbed the dead Confederate under the armpits and dragged him to the wall, laying him next to another dead Confederate. Light spilled out the door, illuminating the faces of the dead men. Cian counted them. Five Union and a dozen Confederate. More, he knew, still lay in the yard. He recognized Martin Dutro, Jude Johnson and George Thompson, all men from Company F. Cian squeezed his fists until the ragged nails bit into his palms. The frenzy of rage built in his chest again. He vowed he would get revenge for these men. And for E.D.

CHAPTER TWENTY-SIX
LAMB TO SLAUGHTER

Jemmy Martin
Beard Ranch, Near Galisteo, New Mexico,
15 miles south of Glorieta Pass
March 26, 1862, late afternoon

The men marched on, leaving San Antonito behind and moving out of the mountains on a long, gentle slope. They wound through another pass, dropped down its north face, and camped in the sleepy little farming community of Galisteo. The village didn't have much going for it except for a sweet-watered stream and the fact that it was just one day's march from Santa Fe.

Willie looked up from the stick he was whittling into shavings. "I's hungry."

"The bummers've been out looking for supplies since noon. They'll be back soon." Jemmy placed an ear on Willie's chest and listened. "I hope we gets orders to move on soon. After so much time in the snow, yer not the only one's developed a cold. We'd all benefit from a bed in a warm house, like we had in Socorro."

A group of bummers, soldiers who had gone out foraging for supplies, came in and set down sacks of cornmeal near the fire. "Lookie what we bummed off a house over yonder. Figger we kin make some Dixie corndodgers to go with the mutton that's coming," one of the men said.

"We got mutton?" one of the men around the fire asked.

Before anyone could answer him, another group of foragers herded in a small flock of scrawny sheep.

"We got mutton!" the man at the fire shouted.

One of the bummers who'd herded them in chuckled. "Paid good Confederate scrip for 'em, too."

Jemmy snorted. Paying in Confederate paper money was like paying with rags. Plus, the tear tracks on the faces of the ragged, dirty boys who had followed the bummers and now stood on the edges of the crowd made him wonder if the people who were paid for the sheep were actually the people who owned them. He jerked his chin towards them. "Anybody asked these boys who the sheep belonged to?"

"Nope," the bummer said. "Anyhoo, they're ours now." A few men fell to skinning and gutting the sheep.

"Least we kin do is give them the skins. Might keep them warm. Or, maybe their Mas know how to card and spin it," Jemmy said handing the wooly skins back to the boys who hovered on the edges of the fire circle. The bulging sides of some of the old ewes told Jemmy that lambing time was near. A man slit the belly of one of the ewes and a lamb popped out and staggered about on unsteady legs, making the men laugh.

"They kin have this little one, too," Jemmy said as he scooped up the lamb. He handed it to one of the boys, who ran back to his village with it. "We's taking so much from these people. A lamb might help them reestablish their herd."

"Spoils of war," one of the men around the fire said.

War spoils everything, Jemmy thought bitterly. He looked after the retreating boys, wishing he could show them how to take an old milk bottle and a rag and feed a newborn lamb. He knew he didn't have the Spanish words to do so. Maybe they knew it as well as he did. Farm boys were farm boys, no matter what language they spoke.

The mutton hung over the fire and corn dodgers sizzled in mutton fat when Willie pointed a finger north at a dust cloud moving south down the road toward them.

"Hell's a brewing, and not a mile off," one of the men muttered.

They all fell silent, waiting to see what was coming their way.

A few minutes passed before Colonel Scurry walked through the line, slapping his hat against his thigh and shouting "Pack up, boys. Major Pyron is in a fight with six hunnert Yankees and has got a truce until twelve o'clock tomorrow, so we must get to him."

Jemmy felt Willie stiffen. He rubbed his hand over the boy's inky black hair. "Little one, your arm is in a sling. You cannot drum, so the Colonel will not put you in the fight."

Willie twisted his head around and looked up at Jemmy with dark eyes sunk deep into his pale skin. "Then, what are we going to do?"

"We will grab meat in one hand and corn dodgers in t'other, and walk tonight. Tomorrow when the fighting starts, we will stay with the supply wagons and medical tents. We'll nurse the sick. Now, let's pack up."

In ten minutes, Scurry's men were on the dark road and heading for the base of Glorieta Pass.

CHAPTER TWENTY-SEVEN
FINISHED

Cian Lochlann
Pigeon's Ranch, Glorieta Pass
March 26, 1862, late evening

Cian woke with a start, almost falling from his chair. For a moment he forgot where he was. It was the groaning of the men lying on pallets and blankets throughout the room that reminded him that he was in the main room of the Inn at Pigeon's Ranch, and it was the evening after the Battle for Apache Canyon. He got down on his knees and studied E.D. carefully. His friend's chest rose and fell, his face wrinkled as if he were having a bad dream or fighting pain. Cian laid a hand on E.D.'s forehead.

E.D.'s eyes fluttered open. "I feel like the whole Union

Army marched over me. Where am I?"

Cian smiled. "At Pigeon's ranch. You had a fall. Nothing that rest won't help. Would you be wanting me to read to you, to help pass the time? What were you reading?" Cian looked around, wondering if his friend's saddlebag was close by. E.D. had the heaviest one in the company. While some men carried extra socks or daguerreotypes of their loved ones, his was filled with books. It was the one regulation E.D. didn't follow.

E.D. let out a long sigh and closed his eyes. "I am finished."

"Don't you be saying such things! You aren't going to die! Not you. You can't." Cian struggled to keep his voice from shaking. Thinking, he remembered his mother saying, is believing.

A tired smile tugged at E.D.'s lips. "That is not what I meant. I mean, I've finished reading all the books I brought with me. And do not search for my saddlebag. I left it at Kozlowski's."

"Ah," Cian said with a sigh of relief, "Then I'll be asking Pigeon in the morning if he has any books lying around that he can lend me. Perhaps I can find something new for you."

The door opened and two stretcher bearers carried in yet another man. They had been doing this all evening, and each time Cian had looked, then looked away. This time, it was William Marshall, the man who, back in Colorado, had won Company F's election for first lieutenant. His election had dropped Luther Nelson down to second lieutenant and George Wilson to First Sergeant. Cian frowned. Even if he didn't like the man, he didn't wish him any harm.

Cian turned back to E.D. "Did you really mean it when you said I could milk a cow if I came and visited your farm?"

E.D. laughed, then winced. "Middle of a war, and all you can think about is milking a cow?"

"Not really. I was thinking about running the farm with you. You be the brains; I shall be the brawn. Tell me what to do, and I will do it. At least, until you are healed up."

E.D. smiled drowsily. "That would be nice. But once I find a wife, you shall have to move to the bunk house."

"We will cross that bridge when we come to it," Cian said, then winced, remembering the bridge over the *arroyo*, and the jump that everyone except E.D. had managed. He worried that the memory would disturb his friend, but E.D. had already fallen asleep.

A little after midnight, George Wilson staggered in and dropped heavily next to Cian. "I heard you was here. I been burying the dead and bringing in wounded. Working side by side with Rebs."

"Really, now?" Cian raised his eyebrows, encouraging George to explain.

"Really. They came in under a flag of truce and asked to bury their dead. They helped us, we helped them. Even loaned them shovels. Funny how friendly men can be when they are not shooting at each other." George held out a flask and Cian took a swallow, then nearly spat it out. It wasn't water.

E.D.'s voice sounded shaky. "That what I think it is?"

George jerked in surprise. "Why E.D.! You're awake! Good to see! Yep, take some, I'll take the edge off." He passed the canteen and E.D., who rarely drank, took a big swig.

As George slipped the flask into his pocket, Cian pulled him aside. He jerked his head over to the corner, where William Marshall was groaning loudly, then whispered so that E.D. couldn't hear. "Did you see who they brought in?

I do not remember him being down in the fight."

George shook his head. "The Lieutenant was supervising a detail of men collecting abandoned Confederate arms. Some of the pieces were old—really old. There were guns from the War of 1812, and squirrel guns and whatnot. I heard he picked up a piece by its muzzle, hit it against a stump, and the thing discharged right into his stomach."

Cian shook his head. "Jaysus. Tough luck." He glanced over at E.D. in time to see his friend wipe away a tear. He was glad he hadn't let E.D. know about Marshall. He had pain enough of his own to hear about other people's.

"Anyhoo," George continued, "some New Mexico Volunteers and Federal infantry have joined us since the sun set. Good to have reinforcements. Some of them, being fresh, have been dispatched to the battlefield to maintain a line of defense, so we do not have to be so on guard here. And scouts found a stash of Rebel supplies. The cooks're working on a feast for us out 'a them. Want me to bring you two a plate?"

"Mary and Joseph! Why didn't you say so earlier! I could eat a horse!"

E.D. groaned and waved his hand dismissively. George nodded and headed out. Cian got up to stretch his legs. He had grown stiff and sore, but looking around, knew he had nothing to complain about. He passed William Marshall, who was moaning more quietly now, his eyes rolled back in his head. Gut-shot, Cian knew, was almost always fatal.

A hand grabbed Cian's ankle. Cian looked down at a Confederate Lieutenant with a bandage wrapped around the side of his head. His blue eyes were so wide that the irises were ringed with white, and his hand shook. There was something spooky, unnerving about the man. Perhaps the head wound had addled him. "Was you one of them riders what jumped the *arroyo*?"

"What if I was?"

"That Major what led y'all: He ain't human. I emptied three revolvers at him and he came through unscathed. So, I ordered my company to fire a volley at him. Nothin' stopped him. Nothin'. He must be the Devil from Hell hisself."

"Or an avenging angel sent from God." Cian pulled his leg out of the man's grip and went back to E.D., but his mind kept wandering back to Chivington.

Chapter Twenty-eight
Sisyphus

Jemmy Martin
7 miles south of Glorieta Pass
March 27, 1862, before daybreak

Lt. Col. William R. Scurry rode his mount up and down the line, shouting encouragement. "Put your shoulders into it, boys! Pyron and his boys need us!"

Grunting, the men heaved against the back of the medical wagon to free it from the half-buried boulder that had stopped it halfway up a hill. Jemmy moved toward the mules who strained in their harnesses, their hooves sparking as their shoes struck rock. He slipped in between them and leaned into the hill with them. "That a ways, you two Johnnies. You kin do this," he muttered to them.

"Which of 'em is Johnny?" Willie asked.

Jemmy looked down and found Willie standing right in front of him. Quickly, he let go of the mule's harnesses, grabbed Willie up in his arms, and ran to the side of the road. "Willie, when that wagon breaks lose, no telling where it's going. You cain't be standing in front of it."

Jemmy set Willie on his feet. His heart pounded as he though of what might have happened.

"But which of 'em is Johnny?" Willie asked.

Jemmy took a deep breath to calm his nerves. "If'n you don't know a male mule's name, he's John. A mare mule is Molly. That's just the way of it. Now, why don't I put you on one of the Johnnies so you don't get run over."

Willie shook his head. "Nope. I ain't never been on a horse and I don't intend to do so now. They's big beasts, and scary."

Jemmy sighed. "These mules are too plumb tired to stir up a fuss. That's why us men are dragging cannons and wagons up and down hill. You'll be fine riding one."

"Nope," Willie crossed his arms over this chest and tucked his chin in under them.

"How 'bout riding in a wagon, with the supplies then? I don't want you underfoot."

"I'll agree to that."

Jemmy caught Willie under the armpits and swung him onto the medical wagon. "He's light," Jemmy said, hoping the men wouldn't mind this little bit of extra cargo. No one argued.

Jemmy walked along beside the wagon. When they crossed yet another *arroyo*, the loose gravel seemed to suck the wagon into it. Jemmy reached under the wagon and pulled up, trying to keep the axles from bogging down. He noticed that Willie, lulled by the rocking of the wagon, had fallen asleep.

The next time the wagon began climbing a hill, Jemmy joined the men pushing on the back of the wagon bed.

"I feel like Sisyphus," the man next to Jemmy said through his grunts.

"Who's sis?" Jemmy asked.

"No one's sis. Sisyphus. He was a Greek. The gods punished him by making him roll a huge boulder up hill. Only he never makes it to the top."

"What was he being punished for?"

"Don't know. But he never completed his punishment. Never made it to the top."

"He must of done something really bad," Jemmy said.

The man grunted. "What'd you do to deserve this?"

Jemmy stopped talking. For a moment, he stopped pushing as he considered the question. What had he done to deserve going to war? Nothing. But here he was. And the longer it went on, the more he thought this man might be right and it would never be over.

They reached the top of the hill and the wagon bumped and clattered down the other side. Jemmy leaned back his head and took a deep breath. A waning moon hung in an eastern sky that was beginning to blush. Although the sun hadn't broken the horizon, its rays caught the bald, snow-covered peaks of the Sangre de Cristo Mountains in front of him.

"Will you look at that?" Jemmy said. "Them's the biggest mountains I ever seen. I don't see how no Union Army is going to march over those."

"Not over. Through," one of the other men who'd pushed the wagon said.

"Through? Like in a tunnel?" Jemmy asked.

The man laughed. "No tunnel. A pass. Glorieta Pass, to be specific. I took the Santa Fe Trail through it once, before the war." As they neared the foothills, Jemmy saw smoke rising from the chimneys of Santa Fe, ahead to the northwest. The Santa Fe trail wound its way northeast, into a gap between the mountains on the left and a flat-topped mesa with steep, rocky sides on the right.

"We've got a little ways, and then we're there," the man told Jemmy. "Johnson's Ranch, where our army's encamped, is at the base of that mesa, where the road starts to climb into the pass."

A little ways, Jemmy thought. And then what? Not the rest in Santa Fe that he'd been anticipating, but another battle. But this time, he and Willie would stay back with the wagons, where it was safe. This time, he'd threaten no one and no one would threaten him or Willie. He was sure of it.

CHAPTER TWENTY-NINE
THE ENEMY

Jemmy Martin
Johnson's Ranch, Glorieta Pass
March 27, 1862

An hour after sunrise, Jemmy staggered into Johnson's ranch. He passed a stable and a few outbuildings, then eyed men clustered around breakfast fires in the yard of a long, low adobe building, looking for anyone he knew.

Willie sat up in the back of the medical wagon, rubbing his eyes. "Are we there yet? I's hungry."

Jemmy lifted Willie out of the wagon. "Yes, Willie. We's here. You feeling good enough to be hungry? That's a good sign. Go find something to eat while I help park this wagon. I'll catch up with you after I get the mules settled."

He gave Willie pat on his backside, and the boy scurried into the crowd, using his nose to guide him to the best fixings.

"Get that wagon in line with those others," a sergeant barked, pointing to a line of wagons along the mesa's edge, "then take yer beasts back there."

Jemmy squinted down the canyon. "Back where?"

"There's a natural corral at the foot of a slide area back in there. It's about half a mile from camp. You can't miss it."

Jemmy unhitched the mules and curried them down before he led them where the sergeant had indicated. The corral, he found, was nothing more than a box canyon, walled off with piled-up tumbleweeds. He pulled a few tumbleweeds aside, led the mules in, then piled the weeds back before standing back and studying the situation. Would a few weeds really keep the hoofstock from bolting? He supposed it would if the horses and mules were as tired as he was. He plodded back through camp, his head so hazy with exhaustion that he gave up trying to get a feel for the lay of the land. Men shouted greetings to friends they hadn't seen since the Army split in Albuquerque. Jemmy ignored them. All he wanted to do was find Willie, then find a quiet place where he could sleep.

"Jemmy! Jemmy! Look who I found!" At the sound of Willie's high-pitched voice, Jemmy's head swiveled to the right. Willie sat with John Norvell and Frederick Wade.

John Norvell waved a bandana, a smile as wide as a Texas sunset warming his face. "Ho, Little Britches! You look like the walking dead!"

"A lot's happened since the last time I seen you two. It's done tuckered me out."

Frederick Wade, the older school teacher turned soldier, stroked his mustache and gave a quick nod of recognition. "Willie here's been filling us in on the details. Says you saved his life with honey and whiskey."

Jemmy dropped into the dirt next to them. "I helped him, maybe, but he would'a pulled through without me. His chest never got rumbly," Jemmy answered.

Wade nodded, looking relieved. A long look passed between Wade, Norvell and Jemmy, each of them remembering William Kemp and the dozens of other comrades buried by the side of the trail.

Jemmy leaned forward and sniffed the air. "Got enough in that skillet to share?"

"'Course we got enough for you." Norvell poked at the skillet's contents with a spoon, releasing a spattering of grease. "Johnson, the owner of this fine establishment, is a Union man. He and his kin skedaddled as soon as he heard we were coming, so we helped ourselves to his larder. We got us bacon and grits and cornbread and beans."

Wade pointed a finger at the boulders high up on the northern slopes. "He is probably up there, watching us and seething about how his food is supporting enemy troops."

Jemmy's eyes scanned the slope. "You think he will try and take it back? Think he got Union soldiers up there with him?"

Frederick Wade shook his head. "Not when the entire Confederate Army is in his yard. And he cannot have many soldiers with him, if any. This pass is rugged, the cliffs steep enough that men would have to crawl up them. And there is little in the way of cedar brush or boulders to hide behind. I tell you; Thermopylae has nothing on this place."

"I do not see what thermometers got to do with mountain passes," John Norvell said.

Wade waved his hand dismissively. "Thermopylae is a mountain pass in ancient Greece, where the Greeks fought the Persians, you numbskull."

"Glad we didn't have to use ancient grease for these grits." Norvell banged his spoon into the mush in the skillet, breaking up lumps while Wade shook his head and muttered about illiterates.

Jemmy laughed. "How've you put up with him, all this long haul?"

Wade waggled his bushy eyebrows. "I am a man of infinite patience. But John, here, seeks to go beyond infinity."

John Norvell laughed aloud. "Let's lick this here skillet clean."

Afterwards, when the food had revived Jemmy, Norvell took him on a tour of the camp. The hospital area, a group of tents near the ranch house, housed about eighty men who were either sick or casualties of yesterday's fight Norvell suggested that Jemmy bring Willie here, but Jemmy decided he could nurse Willie on his own just as well as the doctors in the hospital tents could.

Nearby, a group of Union prisoners of war lounged beneath a canopy of cottonwoods on the banks of Galisteo Creek. A six-pounder cannon sat atop a hill on the south end of camp. It pointed up the canyon to thwart anyone coming down the trail. At the base of the mesa, Scurry's drivers were adding their wagons to the ones lined up wheel to wheel.

"I think I should check on the mules," Jemmy said, heading toward the rockslide.

"Your mules aren't there, you know," John said.

"I know," Jemmy answered. "These that're left might not be mine, but they still need someone to care for them."

They stopped at the edge of the corral. Norvell put one foot on a rock and studied the emaciated animals. "They're a pitiful sight. We started with thousands, and what we got left?"

"Five hundred, maybe," Jemmy said. "Seeing their ribs

and spines like that makes my heart ache. How low we have fallen."

"But we shall rise again," Norvell answered. "We beat 'em at Valverde. We took Albuquerque and Santa Fe with nary a shot. We did not expect to meet any bluecoats here in the mountains, but the fight yesterday showed that they are just a small, advance party. Once we clear them out, we have a straight shot to Fort Union, which is piled high with all the goods we could ever want. And all the fodder these horses need to regain their strength. All we have to do is take the fort and the whole west is ours."

Jemmy glanced sideways at his friend. "You believe that?"

"With my whole heart."

"When is the next battle coming?"

Norvell shrugged. "Should be today, now that you are here with all of Scurry's reinforcements."

They headed back to camp, where Jemmy lay down to get what sleep he could. The day passed quietly, the men nervously waiting for the call to shoulder arms and move. It never came. By nightfall, Jemmy was hoping that both sides had decided the war was over and he could go home.

The next morning, Jemmy watched Colonel Scurry's men move up the trail. He kept his eye on Wade and Norvell until they blended in with the others, then watched until the last man rounded a bend and disappeared from sight. No one remained in Johnson's Ranch but the sick and wounded, those who cared for them, the Union POWs, and the teamsters and packers.

"What are we going to do if the Yanks come now, Jemmy?" Willie asked in a tense voice.

"It's a narrow canyon," Jemmy replied. "Before the Yanks can get to us, they've got to go through Scurry's men. Then, see that cannon? It's pointed directly at the trail, and Lucius Jones, Scurry's chaplain, is in charge of the crew that mans it. He's going to make sure we see no blue uniforms here."

Still, even though Jemmy knew he had nothing to fear, a sense of irrational dread roiled deep in his belly.

Chapter Thirty
Over the Top

Cian Lochlann
Pigeon's Ranch, Glorieta Pass
March 28, 1862, early morning

Cian jolted awake in his chair. He peered around the dimly lit room for a moment before remembering that he was still sitting next to his friend, E.D. Pillier, in the main room at Pigeon's Ranch. Around him lay the other men wounded at the Battle of Apache Canyon. William Marshall, the Lieutenant who had accidentally shot himself while collecting abandoned Confederate arms, had died at dawn the day before. Other men had also died: Some slipping quietly into oblivion, others shouting profanities or crying for their mothers. E.D. had passed a second restless night, thrashing, then groaning in pain whenever he thrashed. He lay so still that Cian cautiously laid a hand on his friend's forehead. It blazed under his hand.

"Jaysus, E.D. Do not get a fever and die on me," Cian whispered. He pulled his hand away, made a fist, and pounded it into his thigh, hoping the pain would blunt his fear of losing E.D. He punched his thigh again and again, his anger growing white-hot. So many good men, dead or injured by that rabble of no-account rebels! He would avenge his comrades today at dawn.

"Key?" Cian felt a hand clasp his shoulder. He looked up and saw the dim outline of George Nelson in the darkness. "Key, it is three in the morning. Chivington's unit leaves at half past four. Do not worry yourself over E.D. I promise I will not leave his side."

Cian stood and stretched his stiff muscles, then went out, saddled Henrietta, and rode back towards Kozlowski's Ranch. At the end of the Battle of Apache Canyon, Chivington had withdrawn back to Kozlowski's Ranch, where he joined up with Col. John P. Slough and his contingent of 900 men. Some of the wounded, like E.D., remained at Pigeon's Ranch. Others, like Sam Cook, had been carried to the Kozlowski's. The men from Cook's company, leaderless because of his injuries, were split up, filling the ranks of other companies. Luther and George were staying at Pigeon's, but Cian had been reassigned to Captain Samuel Logan's B Company, and they were at Kozlowski's.

It seemed like a lifetime since Cian watched Logan climb to the roof of a Denver mercantile store to rip down a Confederate flag. Logan looked like Cian's father, but had a hot temper. Cian smiled an ugly smile. Logan was the perfect leader for him. He was in a hot temper himself, and spoiling for a fight, and Company B always seemed to be in the thick of it.

He arrived at Kozlowski's ranch in time to see men kicking out their fires and mounting up. Men from Ford's Independent Company, the 5th U.S. Infantry, and some companies of New Mexico Volunteers formed up among the Colorado Volunteers' Company B. He noticed a dark little man in a New Mexico Volunteers uniform conferring with Chivington and the other officers. Cian threaded Henrietta through the milling troops until he was near the New Mexico Volunteers.

"Who is that?" he asked a man in a New Mexico Volunteer uniform. The man turned and looked at him uncomprehendingly.

"*No hablo ingles*," he said.

Cian turned to another New Mexico Volunteer. "Do you speak English?

"Certainly," the man said.

Cian jerked his chin towards the man conferring with Chivington. "Who is that little man next to Chivington? He looks like a child. Or a midget."

The man looked Cian up and down in a way that indicated that Cian was a pot calling the kettle black, and Cian realized that the man he had called a midget was no shorter than he was. "That, my friend, is the legendary Lieutenant Colonel Manuel Antonio Chaves. When he was just a boy, he was the only survivor in a fight against Navajos. He crawled home—200 miles—with so many arrows piercing him that he looked like a porcupine. He defeated the Texans when they invaded twenty years ago, and he would have stopped the Americans when they invaded had not his cousin, General Armijo, surrendered. He fought during the Taos Uprising, and is one of the heroes of the Battle for Valverde Ford. He may be small, but he is very brave. We call him *El Leoncito*, the little lion."

"Impressive," Cian said, his face reddening as he realized how important the man he'd insulted was. There was something about him, some air of authority and assurance, that drew the eye. He didn't seem the least bit intimidated by the fighting preacher's size or the way he shouted everything he said.

"Señor Chaves is going to guide us. He knows this area better than anyone; used to graze sheep here."

"How much of a guide do we need to ride down a canyon?" Cian said with a laugh.

"We are not going down the canyon," the man answered. "We are climbing the mesa and coming down behind the *Tejanos* while Colonel Slough and his men attack their front."

Cian smiled his ugly smile. "Crushing them like a nut in a vise."

The man smiled back. "Exactly."

They followed the Santa Fe Trail west for three miles, then turned into what the New Mexican called San Cristobal Canyon but was little more than a narrow, rock-strewn defile.

Cian reined in Henrietta and stared at the column of men who twisted and turned over and around the rocks. "We're going up there?"

"If you think you and your fancy mule can." The New Mexican smirked, his eyes glinting in challenge. "But I don't know. Perhaps you will have to get off and lead her up, no?"

Cian's hand tightened on the reins. He wanted to hit this man for his impertinence. But this was an ally—he could almost hear E.D. reminding him to rein in his temper.

"Just you watch me," Cian said. He gave Henrietta her head. She had gotten him through a snowstorm, so she could get him up this ravine. He leaned forward in the saddle until her mane tickled his nose. She lunged forward, dodging around the larger boulders and hopping over smaller ones. Stones loosened by riders ahead clattered around them, some of them dangerously close and terrifyingly large. If one hit Henrietta in the leg, it would likely break. Some men dismounted and picked their way gingerly up to the top of Glorieta Mesa, but Cian stubbornly rode on.

When Henrietta reached the top, Cian leaned back and blew out a sigh of relief. She had stumbled more than once, but never fallen. From down below, the mesa top looked flat. As it turned out, it wasn't as flat as he'd thought it would be. The tabletop rolled up and down in wooded knolls. *Arroyos*, some of them very deep, scored the land. Thickets blocked the way. The men zigged and zagged toward the west instead of riding in a straight line. Cian could understand why they needed a guide.

They had ridden about five hours when Chivington called a halt. Like the rest of the men, Cian dismounted. He shook out his legs and slapped his bottom, which had grown sore from the saddle. He watched Chivington pull out an old map, then beckon a couple of captains, including Logan, while he spread the map against his horse's flank. The three conferred over it while Lieutenant Colonel Chaves put up a hand to shade his eyes and studied the terrain. Out of the saddle, *El Leoncito's* head didn't reach the middle of Chivington's chest.

Manuel Chaves pointed and said something in Spanish. Cian searched through the riders until he found the man who had interpreted for him before. "Now what does your little lion say?" he asked.

"If his words interest you, then you should know his name. I have told it to you once before," the volunteer said dryly. "He is Lieutenant Colonel Manuel Antonio Chaves, and he says to look at that one tall peak in the distance. That, and the position of the sun tells him that we are five miles east of Glorieta Pass. We need to continue west."

"Very good." Cian felt his face grow hot. Before he had joined the Army, this man's tone would have driven Cian to use his fists. He wasn't sure if it was the Army's influence or E.D.'s, but he was willing to let this argument pass, but not without a little jab back. "Lieutenant Colonel Manuel Antonio Chaves. I will remember that. I happen to be Private Cian Lochlann, and I hope you remember that."

Cian stuck out his hand. The volunteer scowled at it for a moment before he shook it. Obviously, he, too, was weighing whether this conversation should turn into an argument. "You will never be as important or as big a man as the Colonel, but I suppose I should remember you, Lochlann. I am Montoya. Corporal Antonio Montoya. *Bienvenido*: Welcome to New Mexico. We appreciate you Pike's Peakers joining us."

"Only too happy to help you out," Cian answered. Feeling like he had made his point, he swung back into the saddle as the column moved out over land that seemed trackless and unexplored. For almost an hour the tall peak that Chaves had pointed out hardly seemed to move.

Major Chivington raised his arm, halting the troops. He stood in his stirrups, cocking his head. Off in the distance, Cian heard the faint, rolling echo of cannon fire.

"Sounds like the battle is ahead of us," he murmured.

"These mountains can be tricky," Antonio Montoya said. "Sounds echo down the canyons, like rain in a drainpipe. They are not always coming from where you think."

Cian nodded, remembering times when thunder had rolled down from the mountaintops near his mine. It had sounded so close, yet the storm was miles away.

The Major turned his horse so that he was facing his

men. He pointed his finger at first one man, then another, and finally at Cian, whose chest swelled with pride. He loved when the big man singled him out. It made him feel important. "You, you, and you: Ride forward and scout out what lies ahead. Do not engage the enemy if you should run into him. Report back to me what you discover."

Cian gave a sharp salute and guided Henrietta out of formation. He nodded at the other two men, noting that one was a corporal and the other a private like himself. Together they rode forward, not talking, each leaning forward, concentrating on the land ahead of them. The cannon fire continued to mutter like distant thunder.

One of the men pulled up on his reins, then pointed at a rebel soldier, sleeping, his back against a large boulder. Quietly, the three dismounted. Cian's heart pounded so loud in his chest that he was sure it would wake the sleeping man. "I will watch the horses. You two go get him," he whispered.

"Good idea. Cover us," the corporal said. The two gave their reins to Cian, who wrapped them around his forearm, then shouldered his rifle. His hands shook, and he almost laughed from nervousness. Two days ago, he had ridden through a sea of rebel soldiers, slashing his sword and firing his rifle, and now he was spooked by a lone, sleeping man!

Cian's two companions stood over the sleeping soldier. The corporal gesticulated a plan while the private frowned, uncomprehending, then his mouth went into a little O and he nodded and pointed his rifle at the sleeping man. Slowly and carefully, the corporal reached down and wrapped his hand around the rifle that lay in the sleeping rebel's lap. He pulled it back, waking the sleeper.

"Do not move or I will blow your brains out!" the private hissed.

"Put up your hands!" the corporal yelled.

The rebel's hands jerked halfway up, then stopped as he tried to figure out which command to obey.

"Do not make any sound that may alert your comrades. Who are you and what are you doing here?" the corporal said.

The rebel, who still hadn't figured out whether to put his hands up or not, frowned. "Do you want me to answer or not?"

The corporal smacked the rebel's leg with the butt of his own gun. "Just answer the question."

"Right," the rebel said, "Private Eustice Clampsy, from Mason, Texas. I was supposed to be on sentry duty, but I guess I fell asleep."

"I guess you did," the corporal said. "Where is the rest of the sentry party?"

Private Clampsy shrugged. "There ain't no more. I was the only one."

The corporal nodded. "Then, where are the rest of the rebels?"

"Down there. Leastwise, thems what haven't marched up the Pass." Private Clampsy pointed behind him, where the mesa dropped away. On the valley floor below lay a ranch house with dozens of wagons lined up in neat rows and columns in its yard.

"Jaysus," Cian muttered.

"Lordy," the corporal added. "Now what do we do?"

Cian's mind snapped back into the present. "We do what the Major ordered us to do: We ride back and report what we have seen. And we bring the prisoner for questioning."

"Right," the corporal said. "You ride. We will march this Rebel back."

Cian handed over the reins to the others' horses,

mounted, and galloped Henrietta back across the mesa. He arrived in a cloud of dust, skidding to a halt in front of Major Chivington and Lieutenant Colonel Chaves.

Chivington raised his eyebrows quizzically. "You encountered the enemy's rear guard?"

Cian shook his head. "Major, you've just got to see what's below this next ridge."

Major Chivington ordered the troops to stay put. He and Cian trotted the quarter mile to the mesa's edge, passing the two soldiers who were bringing in their prisoner of war. When they got to the edge, Chivington looked down, then emitted a long, low whistle through his clenched teeth. Cian handed him binoculars, then joined the Major belly down in the dirt.

"There are enough tents for perhaps a thousand men, but the few men I see appear to be largely waggoneers, not soldiers. See those men under guard by the creek?"

Chivington pointed, and Cian quickly said "Yes, sir."

"They're wearing blue. I assume they're our boys, taken prisoner during the fighting two days ago. They'll join in on our side if the fighting goes hand to hand, but they will need weapons. Private, round up a detail to carry down extra arms for them."

"Yes, sir!"

Chivington's binoculars swept along the scene as he continued to analyze. "There is only one gun, that six-pounder cannon atop that hill, and it is pointed up the canyon, not at us. If we can move in quietly, they will not have time to reposition it. And all those wagons! Son, I think they can only mean one thing: We overshot the battle and discovered the Confederate Supply Train. Destroy it, and we destroy any chance the Rebel Army has of continuing north."

Major Chivington glanced at Cian, who nodded,

pleased that this great man would look to him for concurrence. At that moment he felt that he would go anywhere or do anything the Major asked him to. Major Chivington was a man of ideals, and he was not afraid to act on his convictions or speak his mind. Cian remembered watching him leap his horse across the *arroyo* in Apache Canyon, his pistols blazing and a holy fire burning in his eyes. He was the leader that Cian had been seeking ever since Da died, and this was Cian's chance to prove himself in the great man's eyes.

The two scrambled back from the edge, then rode to the others. For the next half hour, Chivington and his officers developed a plan while the men rested on the edge of the mesa and watched the rebels run foot races and play cards in the shade of the cottonwoods, oblivious to the enemy above them. The longer he sat there, the angrier Cian got. His friend E.D. was broken in body, and these Rebels were running foot races as if they were at a Sunday School picnic! It was all he could do not to grab his rifle and shoot down at them.

CHAPTER THIRTY-ONE
DEATH FROM ABOVE

Cian and Jemmy
March 28, 1862

The sun was more than halfway to the western horizon before Major John Chivington threw down the dried piece of grass he'd been chewing on and got to his feet. He stepped back from the edge of the mesa and beckoned his men to join him, then began speaking in his best, most convincing sermon-voice.

"This is not where we are supposed to be, men. Colonel Slough's orders were to drop behind the Confederate army and attack their rear. If we could not find their rear, we were to attack their southern flank. Either way, his plan, to split our force so that we could attack on two fronts, was a dangerous one, a gamble with high stakes. Our scouts indicated that the enemy forces were larger than our own; perhaps a third larger. Being so outnumbered, Colonel Slough may now be regretting not having all of his men in the fray.

"Some men may say that we have failed in our objective today. We have found neither the enemy's rear nor their flank. We have not engaged the enemy, and we have left our comrades to fight on their own. But I do not believe that we have failed. Rather, I believe that God himself led us here to fulfill a greater objective.

"What we have before us is not the Army, but its supply wagons. We were not ordered to attack these. Colonel Slough did not conceive of this possibility. But there they lie below us, with only the lightest of guards protecting them. Men, if we destroy these wagons and the supplies within them, we will have dealt a death blow to the Confederate Army. Even if they defeat Colonel Slough and his forces today, they cannot go on without blankets and tents, food and forage. And if, by the grace of God, Colonel Slough is able to defeat the enemy in the field of battle today, the bedraggled remnant will be completely and totally destitute and unable to rise against us evermore. By leading us here, God has assured us the victory."

Cian's heart pounded. The faces around him looked stern and determined. The men handed their mounts to the few chosen to stay behind and guard them. Cian gathered the guard's rifles so they could be handed to the Yankee Prisoners of War in the valley below. The men spread out along the mesa, then dropped over the edge.

With heart in his throat, Cian slipped and slid down the steep, gravelly slope. If he lost his footing, he would tumble head over heels.

On his right, men stopped atop a rocky cliff. They affixed ropes to a straggly juniper, then rappelled over the side.

To his left, men hesitated on a thin ledge. The whole side of the mountain seemed to crawl with blue coats, all out in the open and exposed on the rocky face. One false step, one accidental shout of fear, and the Confederates below would know that the enemy was upon them. Shooting them off the side of the mountain would be like shooting targets at a county fair.

The butt of the extra rifle slung across Cian's shoulder dug into the slope, throwing him off balance. He bent forward to steady himself, then stepped onto a boulder. It moved. He scrambled back as the boulder careened down the slope, crashing through the underbrush and gathering a dirt avalanche behind it. Cian froze, hoping that none of the rebels noticed.

* * *

On the western edge of the Confederate Camp, Jemmy and Willie sat with their backs against a sun-warmed boulder. Jemmy peeled off his coat, and tried to drape it over Willie, but Willie shrugged it off.

"I'm feeling better. Really, I am," Willie said with a snuffle. Jemmy felt the boy's forehead, then folded his coat and set it carefully on the boulder. He set his hat atop the coat and closed his eyes. Birds twittered in the cottonwoods that lined Galisteo Creek. Strange, Jemmy thought, how all could be so peaceful here, when a few miles up the canyons a fierce battle raged. Jemmy tried not to think about the battle. He tried to forget the battle that he had been in, the one near Valverde Ford.

Unbidden, images leapt into his mind. Raul disappearing into the river in a puff of smoke when Jemmy pulled the trigger. Flowing blood. The screams of horses.

Jemmy had never understood what drove his Pa to drink when the dark moods overtook him. Now that he had been to war, he did. He vowed to fight the darkness, fight the rage. And, if he ever made it back home to the farm, he would help his Pa fight his own darkness, too.

Willie looked up the canyon, where the trail turned a corner and disappeared into the pine trees. "You think all is well with them?"

When Jemmy turned his head to follow Willie's gaze, a boulder careening down the canyon wall behind him caught his attention.

Jemmy gasped. The slope was dotted with blue-clad figures.

Jemmy leaped to his feet and ran, shouting and gesticulating wildly to the soldiers near the gun. They pulled out binoculars and scanned the hillside. Even without the binoculars, Jemmy saw a dozen men dangling from ropes on the steepest slope. Other men clustered on a ledge like goats.

The gun crew wheeled the gun around and loaded it.

One of the figures on the slope cupped his hands around his mouth and called down to them. "Who are you down there?"

"Texans, god damn you," the sergeant who commanded the gun called back. His face had turned scarlet, and his jaw twitched.

The man up on the hill unsheathed his sword. It gleamed in the sun as brightly as a signal mirror. "We want you," he shouted.

"Come and get us, if you can." The sergeant gave the order, and the gun erupted in a deafening roar. The ball hit the canyon wall above and to the right of the ledge, throwing out a cloud of dirt. The explosion seemed to dislodge the men on the slope. They ran pell-mell down the slope, whooping and hollering. The few remaining on the ledge provided covering fire.

Jemmy slung Willie over his shoulder and raced up the side canyon, following the packers and drivers. The men leaped onto horses and galloped away, trampling the corral and nearly trampling Jemmy and Willie.

"Up you go," Jemmy shouted. He tried to throw Willie onto the back of a horse.

Willie wrapped his legs around Jemmy's waist. He clung to him, wailing piteously.

Jemmy's desperation rose. He found it hard to breathe. "You got to get on a horse, Willie. It's the only way we'll get away. I know ya'll's scairt, but we can do this. I'll sit right behind you. I'll hold on to you."

Willie shook his head. Tears streaked the mud on his face. "You go. They will not shoot the likes of me. I am too small to be a threat."

Jemmy looked back over his shoulder. A curve in the canyon wall hid the camp, but he heard shots and shouting. The men escaping on horseback had to ride back through camp to get to the road. Had they made it? Or had Union soldiers shot them one by one as they passed? Jemmy pulled Willie into a tight embrace. "I ain't leaving you, Willie. There's a fight back there, and I wants no part of it. Not fer you, nor me. Let's hope they don't think to come down this canyon."

Willie waved his good arm dismissively. "Pshaw. They don't want no truck with a little wounded drummer boy and a stretcher carrier."

"You do not know that."

"Sure, we do. We are not worth arguing with. If them Federals come this way, I will show you. I will tell them what's what and they will just ignore us. You mark my words."

Jemmy shook his head and hoped that he wouldn't have to.

* * *

Cian unslung his rifles and half-ran, half-fell down the slope, using the rifles like walking sticks. On both sides of him, men whooped and fired their weapons. The camp below erupted into activity. The cannon belched flame and smoke. Men scrambled out of tents and buildings, yelling and waving their arms. Horses raced through camp and away toward Santa Fe.

Good, Cian thought. The more men who escaped, the less there would be to shoot at him.

Major Chivington hurtled past, a pistol in each hand, firing as he ran. It gave Cian courage, and he shouted in glee all the way to flat land, where he rallied the men who were supposed to free the prisoners of war.

The camp was a whirlwind of running and shouting men, all shooting at each other. In the heaviest fighting, near the cannon, several rebels fell. A Union corporal hammered a barbed steel spike into the cannon's touchhole, disabling it. The cannon careened downhill, then crashed, shattering the wheels and reducing the caisson to splinters.

A man ran out of a tent waving a white flag. Cian watched him jerk back, shot, the flag swirling around him as he spun toward the ground. He was almost trampled by the Union prisoners of war, whose guard had abandoned them. Cian handed over his extra rifle. His objective accomplished, he moved toward the wagons. He pulled back a brightly-colored Mexican blanket, uncovering a box filled with Colt Navy revolvers.

Cian waved one around triumphantly. "Jaysus! Will you have a look at what is in these wagons!"

"Anything you take, you have to haul up that slope," a sergeant reminded Cian. "Now move. We are placing a keg of powder into each wagon, then we'll set them on fire. Best you be far away when they blow."

Cian jammed the pistol into his waistband. He backed up, nearly colliding with Major Chivington, whose face was flushed, his eyes flashing demonically. "Private, gather some men and find the corral."

Cian pulled himself up to his full height. Even then, he didn't reach the middle of the Major's chest. He was even smaller than El Leoncito. He saluted. "Sir, it is in that side canyon." Cian pointed south.

The Major nodded. "Many of the horses have already escaped. Kill any mounts that remain."

The order shocked Cian. Horses and mules were in short supply. The Union had lost many in the hard march from Denver. Cian swallowed hard, afraid that questioning the command would look disrespectful or, worse, treasonous to the big man who commanded so decisively. "Shouldn't we confiscate them, sir? Do we not need them ourselves?"

Chivington jerked a thumb over his shoulder, indicating the steep slope down which they'd come. "You think we could get them up that? We cannot take them with us, so we shall deny them to the enemy. Destroy their supplies and any means they have to carry newly acquired supplies, and we have destroyed their ability to wage war."

"Yes, sir." Cian snapped a salute, then spun on his heels. He reloaded his rifle, then proceeded up the canyon. If it was empty and there'd be no need to recruit others to do the bloody deed. If it was filled with horses, he'd return and find the toughest men he could find to help him. He had a major to impress.

The side canyon narrowed and twisted. Cian turned

a corner and saw a rustic, improvised fence made of tumbleweeds. Part of the fence lay crushed, and Cian guessed that the escapees had ridden their mounts right through it. A small herd of thin and sickly horses remained. In front of them stood two figures.

Cian slowed. It seemed to him that everyone who could escape had done so on the best of the horses. Those left behind hardly looked worth killing. Neither did the rangy boy wearing tattered homespun or the tiny lad with hollow, haunted eyes and one arm in a sling.

The little one spread his feet in a defiant stance that almost made Cian laugh. "What are you doing here, you filthy Federal?" The voice was high and strident, reminding Cian of the little dogs that Boston women sometimes carried. Those dogs thought themselves fierce, but one kick would send them yelping.

"I plan to liberate the remaining horses from you, Secesh scum," Cian answered.

"And how're you planning on doing that?" The lad shook his fist.

Cian cocked the rifle, hoping the ominous click would send this little strip of a lad yelping behind the bigger boy's legs.

The lad stepped forward. "You will have to get through me first."

"Fine," Cian lowered his rifle. He pulled the trigger.

The boy pitched onto his back and lay there, still and silent. The boy's eyes were open, but the eyeballs had rolled back so that only the whites remained. His mouth was open, his tongue lolling out.

As the dust settled, Cian stared slack-jawed, his heart pounding. He'd wanted vengeance, but on a wee scrap of a lad? What had made him fire on one such as this?

Jemmy dropped to his knees. "He was just a poor orphan boy, with no Ma and Pa." Jemmy said in a voice strangled by his tears. "Why'd you have to go and shoot him?" Jemmy peered at the soldier who stood over him, fiddling with his rifle as if he didn't know how to use it.

The soldier looked no older than he was, his hazel eyes filled with confused vulnerability. The Union soldier dropped his rifle. For a moment he swayed, then his knees buckled and he dropped to the ground, where he sat with a dazed look on his face, raking his hand through his dark hair until it stood on end. "Jaysus, Mother Mary and Joseph. An orphan? Like me."

Jemmy glanced at the soldier sitting beside him and his heart wrenched in agony. He should hate this man, this enemy who had just killed Willie. But Jemmy felt nothing but pity for this boy soldier who was also alone in the world and, judging by his accent, far from home. He hadn't killed Willie out of hatred. The war had made him do it. The war had made many young men into killers. No one, not even innocent boys and beasts of burden, were safe from war's ravages.

Jemmy rested his forehead on Willie's cheek. It was still warm, and made it easy for Jemmy to believe that Willie was still alive. He resigned himself to failure, accepted that war was too big and too powerful for him to thwart. It had taken Golphin and Griffith, his mules. It had taken Willie. War would take him, too, in its own time and on its own terms.

"I suppose you will kill me now," Jemmy said in a matter-of-fact tone.

"Not you. 'Tis the horses I'm after. My major said I needed to kill them all." The soldier held up his hands in a gesture of hopelessness. "An orphan. Jaysus."

"Look at them." Jemmy jerked his chin towards the horses and mules. "Skin and bones. Half dead of malnutrition and overwork. What if we just let them go?" Jemmy tried the even, calm tone that he used when his Pa was drunk and he needed to make his argument sound reasonable. "Loose them. Let the locals gather them up, nurse them back to health. Those that die can at least be eaten. There's not much to eat around these parts. Not with two armies foraging the land."

The soldier snuffled and wiped his snotty nose on his sleeve. His eyes were red-rimmed, but he had yet to cry. "'Tis a box canyon. We free them, they will pass the Major. I will be shot for disobeying orders."

"The canyon's not as boxy as you think. Looky here." Jemmy gently laid Willie's head on the ground. He pulled the soldier to his feet and showed him a makeshift fence of dried cholla stems that blocked a low place in a section of the far wall that had been hidden by a curve and some juniper. "If'n we take down them cactus, there's a back door for 'em."

The soldier pondered for a long moment. Finally, he sighed and nodded. Soon, the corral was empty.

"Now we's got to bury Willie," Jemmy said.

The soldier nodded. "Deep, with rocks on top to keep the coyotes and buzzards away." They turned to walk back across the corral, then stood stock still.

Willie was sitting up, rubbing the back of his neck with his good hand. Cian and Jemmy looked at each other, then back at Willie. They rushed to the drummer boy.

"Am I dead?" Willie asked. "This don't look like I expected heaven to look."

Jemmy burst into tears and he collapsed on to the ground pulling Willie into a tight embrace. "Willie! You had us scairt silly! Where are you hit?"

Willie's one good arm fluttered around, his hand patting his chest. "I don't suppose I am. I don't hurt nowhere.

Must'a passed out."

Cian burst into hysterical laughter. "Jaysus, Mary and Joseph! It's a miracle! The boy's back from the dead!" He wiped the tears from his eyes, grateful that his temper hadn't' cost this boy his life. "But now, what am I to do with the two of you?"

Jemmy shrugged. "Don't ask me. You're the one with the gun."

The soldier shook his head. "I could leave you here, but we've captured your supply train. What will you live on? Come on. You two are my prisoners. That way, you'll be fed and out of the weather. And once you promise not to fight any more, you'll be paroled."

Jemmy looked up, his eyes glimmering with hope. "Paroled? You mean, free to go home?"

Cian nodded. "Exactly."

Jemmy scrambled to his feet. "Come on, Willie! We's getting fed, then we's going home!"

* * *

Cian walked behind Willie and Jemmy as they returned to Johnson's Ranch. His rifle was pointed at them, but he hadn't reloaded it. He eyed his prisoners as he used to study Boston street-urchins. The older one was taller than Cian, lanky and muscular in a loose, shambling way. They would be an even match in a fight. Even so, he wasn't worried. There was something likeable about this rebel, something gentle. The little one was pale skinned, with dark eyes and hair. It was obvious they weren't brothers, but the affection and care between the two touched Cian deeply, and made him think of E.D.

"So, I am called Cian. Cian Lochlann."

The blond boy nodded. "Jemmy Martin, of San Antonio, Texas. Ya'll from Ireland?"

Cian smiled. "'Tis easy to tell, is it?"

"A might. Ya'll talks funny."

A year ago, Cian would have slugged anyone who said such a thing, but now he couldn't help but laugh. "No, friend. You are the one who talks funny. Tell me, Jemmy, are you injured? Why weren't you with the rest of the army?"

Jemmy shook his head. "I ain't no soldier. I's a packer and driver. Only reason I's on this here expedition was to protect my mules, which my brother sold to the army. But my wagon got burned near Valverde and my mules fell into Union hands, so I's been helping with the wounded. Including this here drummer boy with a broken arm. He's Willie."

"I'd figured his name. Surely we can find you a job in our hospitals," Cian said. "We have plenty of wounded, some of them Rebs."

"I'll do what I can," Jemmy said. "But parole! That's what I'm really hankering for."

Boom. Boom. Boom. A series of deep, thunderous percussion echoed off the canyon walls. Cian thought they were the retort of distant guns until a fireball rose over the side canyon's wall.

"Jaysus," Cian ran, forgetting about his prisoners. He cleared the side canyon, and Johnson's Ranch appeared in front of him.

Every wagon was on fire. One had exploded into what seemed like a million flaming bits. Near it, two Union soldiers were dragging a third to safety. Cian saw Antonio Montoya, the New Mexico volunteer who had told him about Lieutenant Colonel Manuel Antonio Chaves. He ran to him.

"What happened?" Cian asked, panting from the run.

The volunteer looked up. "We put a keg of powder in

each wagon, then set the wagons on fire. That one must have had cases of ammo in it. Private Ritter was standing too close. He must be carried back in a litter. Who is that?" he jerked a chin behind Cian, who found the blond rebel and the little dark drummer boy standing behind him, breathing heavily.

"My prisoners," Cian said.

Corporal Montoya pointed to a miserable-looking group of confederates at the far end of the clearing. "Send them there. Captain Lewis is deciding what to do with them."

Cian looked at Jemmy and Willie. He felt a twinge of guilt. He'd captured the two with the intention of saving them from harm. Had he done the right thing? Realizing he couldn't look too friendly with the enemy, he lowered his rifle, pointing it at Jemmy. "Let's go," he said gruffly. Under his breath, he muttered, "You know 'tisn't loaded, don't you?"

"Yes, sir," Jemmy fell into step in front of Cian, one hand up like a prisoner's should be while the other cradled Willie's shoulder.

As they neared the Confederate prisoners, Cian saw the Union prisoners of war that he had freed and armed talking with Major Chivington. They spoke rapidly, gesticulating wildly up the canyon. Cian slowed his pace so that he could hear.

"You had better get away from here quick," one of the men said. "The damned Texans are whipping our men in the canyon like hell, have driven them nearly through the canyon, and pretty soon will have them out on the prairie."

Major Chivington's face clouded. He scowled as he studied the trail that led up into the mountain pass. "This is a precarious situation. By remaining here, we risk getting caught by returning Texans. Captain Lewis, parole those confederates too sick or injured to walk. We will take the rest with us as prisoners of war. I'll need a head count."

"I count sixteen, Major," Captain Lewis answered.

"Eighteen," Cian gave Jemmy a shove forward with the muzzle of his rifle.

Chivington frowned at Willie. "That one looks too little to endure the march. Send him to the Confederate hospital tent there. Line up the rest of them and ready them for the march. If we encounter the main body of Texans, we'll have to shoot them."

Cian watched Jemmy's grip on Willie tighten. He snapped a sharp salute. "Major, sir. Permission to help guard the prisoners."

Chivington nodded. "Granted. Private, have the Confederate mounts been taken care of?"

"Yes, sir. There's not a horse or mule left standing in that enclosure." Cian looked the Major directly in the eye, his gaze not wavering an inch. He told himself he wasn't lying. The horses had been taken care of, even if they hadn't been killed, and the corral was empty.

"How many horses were there?" the Major asked. "A thousand?"

"That's a good estimate," Cian said. Again, he told himself he wasn't lying. It was an estimate. It didn't matter if it was off by, perhaps, nine hundred and fifty.

Chivington's face blazed with an energy that seemed almost supernatural. His nostrils flared; his eyes dilated. It was as if he were burning with the internal fire of his own convictions. He was determined to destroy the Confederate army, whatever the cost. Cian felt a great uneasiness. The man that he had thought he could follow to the ends of the earth was leading him into a hell of destruction. He gathered his inner strength and stared back into those fiery eyes, unwilling to back down.

"Good," the Major said. "I have destroyed the enemy's means to wage war more surely than Joshua destroyed Jericho. Let us move out."

Cian turned back to Jemmy. He leaned close and whispered. "It will be alright. You heard what the Major said. They're paroling all confederates too sick or injured to walk. When you're paroled, you'll be able to come back and collect the boy. And don't worry about being shot. There aren't any Texans where we're going."

Jemmy let loose his grip on Willie, and a medic led him off. Cian watched the boy turn and look at them. Willie's eyes brimmed with tears. Cian swallowed hard and said a little prayer that he was doing the right thing.

CHAPTER THIRTY-TWO
AN ANGEL ON HORSEBACK

Cian Lochlann
March 28-29, 1862

Cian herded the Confederate prisoners up the steep mesa. At the top, he mounted Henrietta, then turned her so that he could watch the rest of Chivington's men climb up. Down in the valley, smoldering heaps marked where the Confederate wagons had been. A few men wandered from body to body, assessing the still forms to decide who needed care and who needed burial. The setting sun dropped below the clouds and lit the whole valley red and orange, the smoke from the wagons reaching into clouds that were looking ever darker and lower. Cian wondered when the storm had moved in. He had been so focused on what was happening on the ground that he had missed what was happening in the air. The sun dropped behind the distant western mountains and the light faded until the scene went indistinct and gray. "Jaysus, Mary and Joseph. It looks like Armageddon down there."

Jemmy nodded. "That's just what your Major wanted: A Confederate Armageddon." Cian gave Jemmy a sharp look, but Jemmy only shrugged. "It's true, ain't it? I saw him, all burning with righteous indignation. He might have been God himself. It ain't so bad. Now, maybe, Sibley will admit defeat and we can all go home."

The column was strung out along the trail, with Cian and a few other riders, including Antonio Montoya, herded the walking Confederate prisoners. In front of him, Chivington rode side by side with Lt. Col. Chaves, the little man who had guided them that morning. They had not gone far when Cian saw a rider approaching from the north. He pressed Henrietta forward, anxious to hear what the rider had to say.

"Lieutenant Alfred Cobb, sir," the rider said, offering Major Chivington a smart salute. "Sir, I left Colonel Slough around midday trying to relay his message to you. I've been wandering atop the mesa for five hours now."

Major Chivington waved his hand dismissively. "And the message? Late as it is?"

"Major Chivington, sir, Colonel Slough regrets having split his forces. The 800 men he commands now face a Confederate force almost twice as large as the one you encountered two days ago. He needs you and your men to join him."

Major Chivington's horse turned skittish, and Cian wondered if it was sensing its rider's annoyance. "If you've been riding around for five hours, I am sure it is too late to save Slough now. Either he's won the field on his own, or he hasn't."

Cian looked into the dark ahead and wondered how far back the Union line had been pushed. He had no doubt that they would be alone up here on the mesa, but would they encounter the enemy when they came down San Cristobal Canyon? Cian noticed that Chivington and Lt. Col. Chaves were arguing with each other. He sidled up to Montoya, who always seemed to know everything "Can you make out what they are saying?"

"Naturally, I can. Your Major wants *Leoncito* to guide us back another way, to avoid Confederates. But my Colonel declines to take responsibility. See, the night is cloudy, moonless, and it may snow soon. If *Leoncito* cannot see the mountains or the track beneath his feet, it will be easy to get lost."

"Then, what do we do?"

"What can we do? We go on."

The men blundered forward for several hours. Their horses snagged themselves in bushes and stepped into holes. Even those who had felt triumph over destroying the Rebel supply depot fell into a grim silence. Cian's heartbeat drummed in his ears. Horseshoes rang on stones. The Union soldier who had been injured in the wagon explosion groaned. "Jaysus," he muttered to himself, "Watch your step, Henrietta. I do not want you to break your leg."

The Confederate prisoners of war stumbled along, just as blind as the men on horseback. It would have been easy for a rebel to slip away in the gloom. None tried. Cian wondered: Were they following along so obediently because they hoped to be fed, or were they as worried about getting lost in the wilderness as he was?

Jemmy's blond hair glowed like molten metal in the faint light. Cian watched the back of his head, which seemed to float through the darkness. What made him so calm in the face of all he had been through? The pale white blur that was Jemmy's hair slipped backwards through the prisoners. Soon he walked beside Henrietta's head.

"You there, Whitey," said the volunteer named Corporal Montoya. "What are you doing?"

"Guiding this here hinny so she don't trip," Jemmy answered.

"Why?"

"I've always been partial to mules," Jemmy said. "Hinnies are right close."

"You trust him around your mount?" Montoya asked. "He's a Texan, you know."

Cian gritted his teeth. "So?"

"So, the Texans invaded us twenty years ago. They are no account. Cannot be trusted."

Cian snorted. "I have heard that said about us Irish often enough, and about you Mexicans, too. I'll be trusting this Texan until he gives me reason not to."

Montoya snorted and jerked on his mount's bridle, moving away as if Jemmy's presence itself was offensive.

Cian smiled and looked down at Jemmy's hair glowing in the dim light. "Where is your hat, Reb?"

Jemmy's hand flew up to his head as if he had forgotten that his hat wasn't there. He let out a little laugh. "I guess in all the hubbub I went and left it back at camp. Forgot my coat, too."

"Your hair almost glows in the dark. Like a *tais*."

"A what?"

"A ghost, I'll be meaning. Or an angel. Are you one or t'other?"

Jemmy shrugged. "Weren't never the superstitious kind, and I ain't religious, neither. Ma took me to church every Sunday, but I guess it didn't stick. I do try to be good, though. Live by the golden rule. That's what Ma wanted."

"Me Mam did the same," Cian said. "I tried when she was alive. But I lost her young, soon after we lost me Da. Been adrift ever since, I have, looking for someone to follow. A strong man. A good man. I haven't found him."

"Not that Major of your'n?"

Cian sighed. "I had thought so. Now, I'm not so sure. Maybe I don't need anyone. I have been on my own, without much help from anyone, including God, for quite some time. No wonder I curse more than I pray." Cian rummaged through his saddle bag, then held out a handful of hardtack. "You hungry?

Jemmy gratefully stuck a corner of the hardtack in his mouth and sucked on it, waiting for it to soften so he could bite into it. "Y'all don't seem like the solitary type to me. Why, I bet you got someone you care about jest as much as I cared about mules an' I care about my Willie."

Cian sighed. "I have a friend. His name is E.D. He was going to teach me to farm after the war. But he was injured in the fight two days ago. I don't know if he'll make it."

"He back at camp?"

"At Pigeon's Ranch."

"I don't know nothing about a ranch for pigeons, but I hope to God you get back to it quickly," Jemmy said. "You needs to be with him, not wandering around out here in the dark. And I needs to get paroled so I can get back to Willie. He may not be as bad off as your friend, but he needs me anyways. I'm taking him home with me. God? You listening?"

No sooner had the words left Jemmy's mouth than tiny flakes of snow began falling. The snow seemed to come together into something that glowed like Jemmy's hair, but was much larger and growing larger still.

Cian blinked. "Jaysus and all the saints. 'Tis the angel Michael come to save us."

"Better than that," Corporal Montoya said as he rode past, "It's Padre Polaco."

"Who?" Cian squinted hard as a pure white stallion that was several hands taller than the other horses appeared out of the darkness. Astride his back sat a big man, with broad shoulders and an air of strength about him that seemed more fitting of a cattle baron than a priest. But Montoya had called this man Padre. Father.

Montoya reined in his horse and turned back towards Cian. "We call him Padre Polaco: the Polish priest. His real name is hard to pronounce. Griz-lack-cow-ski, or something like that. He used to serve a parish down in the Manzano mountains. He left the priesthood and runs a mercantile up in Las Vegas now, but he volunteered to be the chaplain for the 2nd New Mexico Volunteers. All the boys like him. He puts on no airs. Polaco is an old friend of *Leoncito.* He knows this country better than most anyone. If anyone can get us home in one piece, it's him."

Jemmy grinned up at Cian. "The answer to y'all's prayer. Someone to follow."

"For tonight, at least." Cian handed both Jemmy and Montoya a piece of jerky from his saddle bag. The column stepped out with renewed enthusiasm, but the excitement of having a new guide couldn't overcome the exhaustion of the men or the difficulty of moving through rough country in the dark, especially now that the snow was falling. The more time went by, the quieter the men became. What would they find at the end of their journey? The Padre knew the way to Kozlowski's ranch, but even he didn't know if the ranch was still in Union hands. Still, they followed the horse's ghostly glow through ever bigger snowflakes.

Cian shoulders were so tense, they hugged his ears. His hands cramped from clutching the reins. The closer they got, the more he feared that E.D. had died while he was gone. His mind wandered through memories: E.D. teaching him to ride, loaning him books, offering to teach him to farm after the war. The more he thought about it, the more Cian understood that E.D. was the one he had been searching for ever since his Da died. E.D. was not a plotter like Sam Cook. He was no despot like Samuel Logan. He wasn't the charismatic leader that John Chivington was, but neither was he the ruthless fanatic that the fighting parson had also proven himself to be. E.D. was steady and dependable, and even though he was not all that much older than Cian, he had become a father figure, patiently guiding him into becoming a better man. Cian heard a sob and looked down at Jemmy's tear-streaked face. Snow dusted the Texan's blond hair.

Jemmy swallowed, flinching as he did so. His voice sounded gruff and strangled. "Poor Willie. I hope he's not cold."

"How about you?" Cian asked. "You cold?"

Jemmy shrugged and wiped at his nose. "Been cold ever since I left San Antonio."

"Are you sick?"

"Sick of this war," Jemmy answered. They walked along in silence, Jemmy's hand gently cupping the hinny's jaw. Tears streamed down Jemmy's cheeks, but he was silent in his grief.

"I am sorry the Major made us leave your friend behind," Cian said. "You can see this walk would have been difficult for him."

"Weren't ya'lls fault Willie got left," Jemmy said, wiping his nose with his sleeve. "Probably, it were for the best. He was sick. Had a cold I worried would settle in his lungs. I think it was his parting gift to me."

It was well past midnight when the ghostly glow

seemed to disappear into the earth. Padre Polaco led the men down a defile even narrower and steeper than the one they had climbed up that morning. Cian leaned far back in the saddle, letting Henrietta choose her own way down into Glorieta Canyon. When they reached the bottom, Cian saw the familiar fronts of Kozlowski's store and tavern lit by the flickering light of a dozen campfires. Dark outlines of men rolled in blankets littered the ground. Were these men Union or Confederate?

The whispered order to fix bayonets moved back through the ranks. Cian and the other guards circled their mounts around the Confederate prisoners. They were a pitiful bunch, thin and dressed in tattered rags. Still, if the men around the campfire were Confederate, having prisoners might be a useful bargaining chip.

A figure stepped out of the darkness, blocking the campfire light. Cian felt every man around him draw in a breath, waiting to see if this was friend or foe.

"Halt," it called. "Who goes there?"

Chivington didn't hesitate. "Major John Chivington, of the U.S. Army."

The figured relaxed. "Major, sir! We have been anxious for your return! Welcome back!"

A cheer went up from the men around him, the tension melting into relief. They had made it through enemy lines, safe and sound. Cian felt a hand on his knee and looked down.

"Best find yer friend, soon's you can." The words came out strangled. Shivering, Jemmy swallowed, then winced.

"Let me find you a doctor first," Cian said.

The Texan shook his head. "I've caught a chill, I guess. Throat's sore. But that ain't no reason to see a doctor. All I needs is rest, and maybe somethin' warm in my stomach."

Cian swung down from the saddle and placed his

hand on Jemmy's forehead. It was a gesture he remembered from long ago, and it brought back tender memories of his Mam. "Why, man, you are burning up. You need a doctor."

"Don't waste yer time. Find yer friend."

Cian handed Henrietta's reins to a milling soldier and slipped his shoulder under Jemmy's arm. He half dragged; half walked him toward the little shed he'd found the day they arrived at Kozlowski's ranch. "I know just the place for you. It has blankets, and is quiet, so you can sleep. I will leave you my canteen and promise to be back with some stew or soup or something, just as soon as I find out about E.D." He laid Jemmy on the pile of saddle blankets, unfolding several and placing them over the Texan, who muttered something incoherent, then drifted into unconsciousness. Cian set his canteen and a packet of beef jerky on the ground next to the blankets, then pulled the door closed behind him. If thinking was believing, Cian would have thought Jemmy back to health.

Cian talked with the men around a campfire and learned that all but the most seriously wounded had been brought from Pigeon's Ranch and were now here in camp. He made his way to Kozlowski's Tavern, which had been turned into a hospital, but didn't find E.D. No one could tell him if E.D. was at Pigeon's, or buried. The day had been so tumultuous and eventful that no one seemed to know where anyone was.

Cian walked back to the corral. He found Henrietta, her head hanging, clearly exhausted from the long ride through the night. Exhausted himself, Cian couldn't think of any other way of finding E.D. but to saddle her up and ride to Pigeon's Ranch. He apologized to her, promising to give her a whole bag of oats and two full days to rest once he'd found his friend.

As he rode out of camp, Cian thought about all he would tell E.D. He was thinking about how his friend would like to hear about the great white horse that had led them like the pillar of fire had led the Israelites through the wilderness when he saw something glowing white on the ground by the side of the trail. As he drew near, he realized that it was the great white horse. A man holding the reins of a smaller sorrel, knelt at the white horse's head. Even in the darkness, Cian recognized those broad shoulders.

"Padre?" Cian slipped from Henrietta's saddle and knelt with the man who had guided him back to the Union encampment. He placed a hand on the white horse's neck. It was cold.

"He was the best horse I ever had," Padre Polaco said in a deep, strained voice.

Cian leaped to his feet and hugged Henrietta's head. "I am sorry, Padre. Really sorry."

"As am I." Padre Polaco got to his feet and clapped Cian on the shoulder with his strong, broad hand. "I was riding Angelo to Pigeon's Ranch, to check on the wounded. He only made it this far. I will be back tomorrow, and I will get a detail to bury him then. But the men need me. I borrowed this little mare to get me to them. Are you going that way, too? We can ride together."

"I was," Cian said. "My friend, he was wounded in the fight for the bridge over Apache Canyon. But seeing your Angelo makes me worry for my Henrietta here. I'm t'inking trading her for a new mount, like you did, would be wise."

The Padre traded the sorrel mare's reins for Henrietta's. "No, son. I'll take her back for you. You go on. Find your friend. I will be right behind you."

The lump in Cian's throat made it impossible for him to argue.

CHAPTER THIRTY-THREE
FLY AWAY HOME

Jemmy Martin
March 29, 1862

Jemmy curled up in a tight ball and tried to banish the ice from his veins. He had never felt so cold. He tucked his fists into his armpits and pulled his legs up against his body, but his teeth continued to chatter and his whole body shook uncontrollably. His mind moved like a stone skipping over a pond, dropping down into dreams, then coming up into wakefulness, so that the sounds of the camp outside mingled with his dreams. He couldn't tell one from another.

Ma tucked the horse blankets around his shoulders. He was a boy in the log cabin in San Antonio. It was early spring. The warm smell of sun on fresh-tilled earth filled his nose. "Are you burying me? Am I dead?" he asked her.

Her face changed into that of the little Irishman. "I will be back with some stew or soup," the face said before elongating into a mule's face.

"Golphin, girl! I thought I'd lost you." Jemmy rubbed his cheek against the stiff hair of her neck until it folded into a saddle blanket. All went dark. The darkness thickened and he was underwater. Someone was shooting over his head. He dared not surface. His feet burned blue with cold. He could not hold his breath any longer. He screamed. Instead of sound, gun smoke belched from his mouth. He choked on the sulphuric smell.

A fly landed on his face. He tried to flick it off but his fists had frozen to his armpits. Ma had buried him deep. He walked through the dark until he tripped on a root and awoke with a jerk.

Jemmy threw off the blankets with a feverish gusto and sat up. His heart pounded and he was still shaking, his throat so parched that he couldn't swallow. He remembered the Irishman—what was his name? Key Inn?—saying something about a canteen. Jemmy groped around until he found it and a little packet near his feet. Jemmy drank half the water, then fumbled with the packet until he'd unfolded the waxed paper. He broke off a chunk of jerky and stuffed it in his mouth, then curled back into the blankets. Slowly the jerky softened. The saltiness revived him. He dropped into a deep and dreamless sleep.

When Jemmy next awoke, light peeked through the cracks around the door. He sat up and reached for the supplies Cian had left him. He found a handful of dried apples sitting atop the jerky, and the canteen had been filled. Jemmy ate it all, and then leaned up against the wall, wrapping his arms around his legs.

Staring at the rectangle of light outlining the door, he took stock of his situation. He no longer shook uncontrollably, and his body had warmed to a normal temperature. But in spite of feeling better physically, Jemmy despaired. He was a prisoner of war. The Irishman had said that he would be paroled soon, free to go back to the burned Confederate camp and find Willie. But, perhaps he would be placed in shackles and marched north to a desolate, unhealthy prison similar to the one his father had languished in after the failed Texas Expedition. Many of Pa's friends had died in prison. Pa had returned emaciated and broken in spirit. Jemmy closed his eyes. *Please, God,* he thought. *Don't let that be my fate, too. Now that I understand him, let me return home strong enough to help my Pa.*

The door creaked open, flooding the room with light. Jemmy squinted and shielded his eyes. The figure in the doorway was wreathed in light. Mist curled around its head, giving it a ghostly, unnatural aura. Or, Jemmy thought, maybe it was a halo.

"Ah, good. You're awake. I brought you breakfast." Jemmy recognized the lilt of the accent. It was not mist he saw, or a halo, but steam rising from a tin cup that Cian carried. Cian placed the cup in Jemmy's hands. The heat felt so good that he had a hard time letting go to grab the spoon. The smell made his mouth water. He stuck a heaping spoon full of cornmeal mush, gravy, and stewed meat into his mouth and groaned with pleasure, mumbling out a word of thanks.

Cian sat down next to Jemmy. "I am glad to see you feeling better. I have checked on you a few times. You were feverish. Delirious. 'Tis been hard not to call the doctor."

"And your friend?" Jemmy spluttered through a mouthful of breakfast.

"He is much improved." Cian's face brightened.

"I doubt he will ever be fit for service again, though. Tomorrow, the Army loads the wounded into wagons and takes them to Fort Union. Only those they do not dare move will stay behind. With luck, E.D. will go tomorrow. And with more luck, I'll be escorting the hospital train. Maybe they'll be sending us both home."

"Let us hope for that," Jemmy said.

"But here lies the rub." Cian's face settled into a grim seriousness. "The Confederate Army has retreated to Santa Fe. We do not expect another battle out of them. Tomorrow, we transport prisoners of war. North. Away from Texas. We expect the remnant of Sibley's Army will continue south, down the Rio Grande to Texas."

"What about parole?" Jemmy asked.

Cian shook his head. "Maybe they'll parole you later, when the Union is tired of feeding you. But for now, the powers that be have determined that it's too easy for soldiers to rejoin their units and resume the fight. They want Sibley out of New Mexico, or at least heading that way, before they'll parole any more soldiers."

Jemmy leaned his head against the wall and sighed. "I figgered that'd be happening. I am resigned to it."

"Well, if you're resigned, you're resigned. But that will mean that orphan boy of yours will leave, and you may never see him again." Cian's voice trailed off. He drew a second spoon from his pocket and scraped it against the wall. A bit of red dirt littered the blanket. "Have you ever noticed how soft these walls are? Kozlowski did not bake these adobes long enough. Why, you could dig through them with just a spoon."

Jemmy stared at Cian, confused. Cian just smiled back. He tucked the spoon into his pocket, stood up, and took off his jacket. "'Tis a warm day. I won't be needing this, so I'll just be leaving it here. Won't need this cap, either. The camp is busy: Packing up, repairing equipment, making lots of noise. I don't think they would hear a little *scritch scratch* coming from a shed."

Cian walked to the door, then turned back and looked at Jemmy. "That orphan boy? He needs someone to guide him, so he doesn't turn out a ruffian like me. And your family? They need a mule. I'll be riding a borrowed horse to Pigeon's Ranch to check on E.D. now. I can't take my hinny, Henrietta. She needs another day of rest. I won't return until after the sun sets. 'Tis a lot of going back and forth between the camps at Kozlowski's and Pigeon's place. In the dark, 'tis hard to see who is who.

"I'll be taking E.D. home," Cian continued. "Home, Jemmy, to a place I've never been before, but where I expect to get a fresh start on life. If you are lucky enough to have a home and a mother and father, 'tis where you belong. 'Tis where that orphan belongs, too. So, I'll be saying farewell to you, and God bless."

Cian pulled the door closed. Jemmy stared at the bright outline in wonderment. Briefly, he considered whether the Irish boy was leading him into a trap of some kind, but it didn't seem likely. He didn't know why Cian was giving him a chance to escape, but he was sure that was what had just happened. He blinked, then snapped out of his reverie, ate the last of his breakfast, and began scraping at the wall. Hours passed. Jemmy didn't notice anything but the size of the depression in the wall and the pile of dirt accumulating on the blankets. When his spoon broke through, creating a pinpoint of light, he sucked in his breath, listening to see if anyone on the outside noticed.

Jemmy crouched next to the hole, watching the light fade. Evening was coming. When the light outside appeared as dim as the light inside the shack, Jemmy carved out a hole large enough for him to stick his head through and look around.

He felt a warm breath on his neck and froze. Something soft nuzzled his neck, then nickered. Jemmy looked up into the face of Henrietta, the piebald hinny Cian had ridden back from Johnson's ranch.

"What are you doing here, girl?" he whispered. Henrietta nodded her head and nickered again. Jemmy dug until the hole was big enough to shimmy through. He reached back in and retrieved Cian's hat, which he rammed on his head, and jacket, which was tight, but warm. He patted Henrietta and discovered that she was hobbled, her saddlebags full of blankets, food and water. Clearly, she was here for him.

Dressed in a Union jacket, Jemmy rode out of camp, toward Pigeon's Ranch. The moon hadn't risen, and the night was very dark. With luck, he could pass through the lines without meeting anyone. He would stop and collect Willie, then the two of them would make their way to Santa Fe, where he could join up with the tattered remnants of Sibley's Army.

He was nearly to Pigeon's Ranch when he saw a rider coming toward him. Jemmy took a deep swallow to settle his nerves. "Good evening," he said in as deep a voice as he could muster, trying hard to control his drawl.

"Evening," the other rider said as he passed by.

Jemmy sighed. He recognized the lilt of that voice. There was so much he wanted to say, but he touched his heels to Henrietta's sides and carried on.

ABOUT THE CHARACTERS

Some of the characters in this book are based on actual, historical people. John P. Slough. John Chivington, and Manuel Antonio Chaves are well documented. Others, like Sam Cook, Luther Wilson, Samuel Logan and E.D. Pillier, are less famous. I have seen pictures of some of these people. You can see them, too, if you visit my Pinterest page. Others I know only from roster lists or newspaper articles. Cian Lochlann never existed outside my own imagination. Neither did Willie or Jemmy Martin.

The same is true with the events depicted in this novel. Samuel Logan really did pull a flag down from the mercantile building, Sam Cook really did plaster the mining country with recruitment posters, a sentry really did shoot at cattle, thinking they were Confederates, and at least one Confederate prisoner of war dug himself out of his adobe confinement using a spoon.

FOR FURTHER READING

There are many books about the American Civil War, but few mention the war in New Mexico. *Valverde*, the first book in this trilogy has a list of books to read. Here are a few more:

Alberts, Don E. *The Battle of Glorieta: Union Victory in the West*. Texas A &M Univ Press, 2004.

Draper, Kenneth. *The Pike's Peakers and the Rocky Mountain Rangers: A History of Colorado in the Civil War.* Textstream, 2012.

Edrington, Thomas S., and John Taylor. *The Battle of Glorieta Pass: a Gettysburg in the West, March 26-28, 1862.* University of New Mexico Press, 1998.

Hollister, Ovando James. *Boldly They Rode: A History of the First Colorado Regiment of Volunteers*. Golden Press, 1949.

Hollister, Ovando James. *The Mines of Colorado*. S. Bowles, 1867.

Peticolas, A. B., and Don E. Alberts. *Rebels on the Rio Grande: The Civil War Journal of A.B. Peticolas*. Bickerstaff's Historical Publications, 2013.

Scott, Robert. *Glory, Glory, Glorieta: the Gettysburg of the West*. Johnson Books, 1992.

Thompson, Jerry D. *A Civil War History of the New Mexico Volunteers & Militia*. University of New Mexico Press, 2015.

Thompson, Jerry D. *Civil War in the Southwest: Recollections of the Sibley Brigade*. Texas A &M University Press, 2001.

Whitlock, Flint. *Distant Bugles, Distant Drums: The Union Response to the Confederate Invasion of New Mexico*. University Press of Colorado, 2008.

ABOUT THE AUTHOR

Jennifer Bohnhoff has been interested in history for as long as she can remember. When she was in high school, she and a friend scoured the routes the Confederates took, using a metal detector to find artifacts that helped pay for her friend's college. She has walked large portions of the Santa Fe trail and been to almost every old fort in the territory. A native New Mexican, she taught New Mexico History at the Middle School level, supplementing the text with stories of some of the real people that appear in her novels. She made those figures come alive for her students; so much so that one student once asked her if she dated Kit Carson, and another asked her if she witnessed a Civil War battle. Mrs. Bohnhoff lives high in the Sandia Mountains, not far from the village where Jemmy buys the honey for Willie.

Mrs. Bohnhoff is available to give zoom and in-person presentations to classrooms, libraries and adult groups on the historical backgrounds of her novels and/or the writing process.